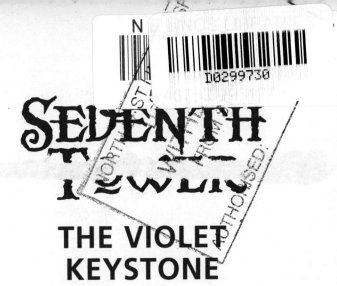

SEVENTH TOWER

THE VIOLET KEYSTONE

THE SEVENTH TOWER

THE VIOLET KEYSTONE

HarperCollins *Children's Books*

First published in the USA by Scholastic Inc 2001
First published in Great Britain by HarperCollins *Children's Books* 2010
HarperCollins *Children's Books* is a division of HarperCollins*Publishers* Ltd,
77-85 Fulham Palace Road, Hammersmith, London W6 8JB

www.harpercollins.co.uk

www.garthnix.co.uk

1

The Seventh Tower: The Violet Keystone
Copyright © 2001 Lucasfilm Ltd. & TM. All rights reserved.
Used Under Authorisation.

Garth Nix asserts the moral right to be identified as the author of this work.

ISBN 978 0 00 726124 6

Printed and bound in England by
Clays Ltd, St Ives plc

THE SEVENTH TOWER sequence is dedicated to the many people at Scholastic and Lucasfilm, in all departments, who have worked so hard; and to the booksellers who have so enthusiastically put THE SEVENTH TOWER books into the hands of readers.

This last book is particularly dedicated to the three people who were essential to the books getting written at all. To my wife Anna McFarlane; my agent Jill Grinberg; and to David Levithan, an editor of the highest level of Violet.

1

Tal returned to consciousness in slow stages. The first stage only lasted a few seconds. He felt himself being carried upside down, his face almost scraping the floor. Then he blacked out again. The next time he came to, he tried to move his hands and couldn't, because they were tied behind his back. He felt sick and threw up. Someone cried out in disgust and hit him, bringing the darkness back.

The third time he regained consciousness, it took Tal quite a while to work out where he was. It was still dark, but not the total darkness of the Ice outside the Castle. There was light not too far away, the constant light of a Sunstone. His arms were no longer tied, but when Tal reached out, he hit something. He tried to stand up and smacked his head. He tried to stretch his legs and couldn't.

Hunched over, Tal felt above his head. His hands slid across smooth crystal, a downward arc.

He was inside a globe. A crystal globe.

There was only one such globe that Tal knew of. He felt fear grab at his stomach and send a shiver down his back.

He was trapped in the punishment globe in the Hall of Nightmares.

Slowly Tal's eyes adapted to the dim light. He could see the outline of the globe around him. Beyond were the silver stands that held the Sunstones that powered the nightmare machine. Those Sunstones were dark now, the machine silent.

Tal heard a door scrape open. A single light flowered in the distance and grew bright. It came from a Sunstone – a Sunstone held in the hand of a man who was feared by all the Chosen, a man whose name was used by parents to threaten rebellious children.

Fashnek.

Half-man, half-shadow. Master of the Hall of Nightmares. A tall, almost skeletally thin man, his long black hair hung in unkempt tendrils on either side of his face. From his left shoulder down to his left hip, Fashnek was made of shadow. Long ago something had bitten away his arm and a good portion of his chest and stomach. He had been kept alive by his Spiritshadow, which had melded itself to his living flesh. Perhaps the result would have been bearable if the Spiritshadow had been vaguely humanoid. But it was not. It was a giant Aeniran insect, with six multijointed legs and a repulsive, elongated head that ended in a ring-shaped mouth, unpleasantly like a leech's.

Fashnek's walk was half a limp and half a slither. Two other Spiritshadows accompanied him, a few paces behind. They had to be free Spiritshadows – supposedly forbidden in the Castle – for there was no sign of their Chosen masters.

One was an Urglegurgle, a creature that resembled a giant upside-down mushroom. It bounced from side to side, occasionally tumbling completely over and snapping its disc-like body together. In Aenir, Urglegurgles dug themselves into soft ground and bounced out upon their prey, completely closing over it, the central "stalk" spraying intensely concentrated acids upon its food. As a Spiritshadow, that stalk might spray a corrosive shadow.

The other Spiritshadow was one of the narrow-waisted, broad-shouldered humanoid creatures favoured by the Empress's Guards. Tal didn't know what they were called.

Fashnek stumbled as he approached the globe that held Tal. Both his human hand and his insectoid shadow pincer grabbed at one of the dream machines, only just arresting his fall. Angrily, Fashnek hauled himself upright and flailed at the Spiritshadows.

"Be careful!" he shouted. "Keep your distance!"

The Spiritshadows retreated a little, even though it had clearly not been their fault.

Tal lay still. The Sunstones around the globe slowly sparked into life, triggered by Fashnek's arrival. The Chosen boy felt sick and disoriented. How had he ended up here?

Slowly he remembered. It was like putting the last few pieces of a light-puzzle together, to trigger the moving image. He had come back from Aenir. The Violet Keystone… Tal surreptitiously looked at his hand. His half of the Violet Keystone was gone. But had Sushin taken it, or had Graile – Tal's mother – somehow managed to get it? He remembered the ball of water-spider poison Sushin had thrown at him. Tal had said something to Graile then. But what? Had she managed to pretend she was still in a coma?

Someone must have given him the antidote to the water-spider poison though or he would still be unconscious. Or perhaps the poison was weaker when it wasn't injected by a spider's hollow fangs.

Fashnek stopped, clattering into one of the Sunstone stands. He was either drunk or very nervous, Tal realised. This gave him some heart. Surely if his jailer was nervous that was good news for him.

Fashnek kept looking over his right shoulder, the human one. His nervousness was contagious too. The Spiritshadows kept looking back towards the door.

Tal kept his eyes narrowed to slits so he looked like he was still unconscious. He desperately wanted to look around, because he could feel his own Spiritshadow – Adras – somewhere nearby. But that would not be wise. Better to lie still and hope for the chance to surprise Fashnek.

There was a knock at the door. Fashnek jumped and the two Spiritshadows rushed back towards the sound. The door opened before they could get there and a Chosen guard stepped in, his Spiritshadow close behind him.

"What news?" shouted Fashnek, almost toppling over as he swung around.

"The enemy is in the Red levels, but we are holding them there," said the guard confidently. "Sushin wants to know what you have learned from the boy about these... Icecarls. We need to know their weaknesses and how to recognise their leaders."

"I... I have not yet begun," answered Fashnek. "It is not easy..."

"Hurry, then," said the guard. "The Most Violet Sushin desires a report from you within the hour."

With that, the guard turned and left the Hall, slamming the door behind him.

"Most Violet? Most Violet?" muttered Fashnek. "Now is not the time to take on such titles."

Tal watched as Fashnek hobbled closer to the globe, his human hand fumbling to draw a Sunstone out of the pouch he wore at his waist. So Sushin had declared himself *Most Violet*. That had to be a step towards letting the Chosen know the Empress was dead and declaring himself Emperor. Perhaps Sushin needed to do that in order to wield the Violet Keystone, the Keystone he would use to deactivate the Veil that protected the whole world from the Sun – and from the Aeniran shadows who Sushin ultimately served.

Tal had to stop Sushin. He almost laughed at himself as that thought struck home. Here he was trapped inside a crystal globe in the Hall of Nightmares and his overriding emotion was not fear but cold rage, a desire to escape and take on Sushin; his master, the Spiritshadow Sharrakor; and all the shadows of Aenir.

Fashnek moved one of the Sunstone stands. The

stands ran on rails set into the floor, so they could be slid into different positions. Tal stared at the stones as Fashnek moved the stands closer. He could feel the power of the Sunstones deep inside himself, in a way he had never felt before. Tal recognised the unusual nature of these Sunstones, which had been so ill-used for so long. They were tainted with nightmares, fear and pain. But he could use them for a while.

It was like a sixth sense. He knew he could reach out to them mentally and try to take control of their power.

Controlling distant Sunstones was the highest feat of Chosen Light Magic. Controlling someone else's stones was unheard of. But Tal knew he could do it. After all, even though the Violet Keystone had been taken from him, wasn't he the newly anointed Emperor of the Chosen, even if it was only in name?

Tal focused on the nearest stone. He would make it pulse, just to know he had control. He felt its steady blue light, reached out to it with his mind, and...

It pulsed. Once... twice... three times.

Now he knew he could wrest control of the stones and release himself. He remembered the light sequence Ebbitt had used to release Milla. All he had to do was reach out now to the other stones. Adras was somewhere close. With his help, and the element of surprise, Tal could take on Fashnek and the Spiritshadows.

Tal sighed in relief.

That was a mistake. Fashnek looked quickly over and his human hand shot to a small bronze wheel set in the side of one of the dream machines. The wheel spun easily.

There was a hissing noise at Tal's feet and he smelled something sweet and sickly. He remembered what Milla had told him of her experience in the crystal globe.

Knockout gas!

Sure enough, a thick green gas had begun to waft about his feet. Tal held his breath and concentrated fiercely on the Sunstones. First one, then another came under his control. Sweat broke out on his face as he held them, changed their colour, and moved on. Three Sunstones... four

Sunstones... there were seven needed to release him.

Tal's lungs hurt. He desperately needed to breathe. Five Sunstones, their colours winking. Fashnek was turning the wheel madly and more gas was flooding in. The Spiritshadows were closing, circling the globe.

Six Sunstones. Tal reached for the seventh. There was a terrible, stabbing pain in his head. He gasped with the pain and took in a breath.

For a fraction of a second, all seven Sunstones were under Tal's control. But the colours were wrong and, in that single second, the gas did its work.

Tal slumped to the bottom of the crystal globe. The seven Sunstones changed back to their normal colours.

Fashnek wiped a sheen of sweat from his forehead with his good hand and looked in every direction, as if seeking some escape. But there was no escape. Sushin demanded answers and there was only one way Fashnek could get them.

Slowly he approached the crystal globe, a

Sunstone held high in his right hand while the shadow pincer that took the place of his left arm slid through the crystal. Fashnek hesitated for another few moments, the Spiritshadows beside him moving restlessly. Then his shadow pincer moved again and cupped Tal's head.

2

Milla Talon-Hand, War-Chief of the Icecarls, let her hand fall wearily to her side. The Talon of Danir she wore on one finger, which had only moments ago lopped the head off a Spiritshadow, shrank back to the size of a long nail. Only the glitter of light in its crystal shape hinted at its temporarily dormant powers.

"They have fallen back, at least for a time," reported Saylsen, the senior Shield Mother. She lifted her face mask to speak, revealing a scarred and battered face and eyes that had seen thirty or forty circlings of battle out upon the Ice. But nothing she had seen before had equipped her for fighting in the Castle of the Chosen, where their enemies wielded Light Magic and Spiritshadows stalked through floors and walls and doors. "What is the War-Chief's will?"

Milla looked around at her exhausted and diminished band. It included her own Spiritshadow, Odris, a unique companion for an Icecarl. As usual, Odris was keeping her distance from the shadow-slaying Talon on Milla's hand. Then there were Shield Maidens and Icecarl hunters, and the seemingly unkillable Sword Thane Jarek the Wilder, a berserk warrior whose skin was bright blue. The colour came from soaking in Norrworm blood, which had transformed his skin into something tougher than Selski armour, save for an irregular patch around his eyes, nose and mouth. Jarek was shirtless, his trousers another sign of his victory over Norrworms, since they were made of the creatures' scaly skin. His chosen weapon was a chain of golden metal that he wore twined around his waist when it was not in his hand.

He was sitting cross-legged and blank-eyed now, in the aftermath of his battle fury. It had left as rapidly as it had come, or he would still be chasing Chosen. Jarek was scratched and burned in a dozen places, particularly around his face. The Chosen had eventually realised they would have to put a Red Ray of Destruction through an eye or his open mouth to kill him.

It was Jarek who had got them into their current predicament, though Milla had seen it as an opportunity at the time. After his companion, Kirr, had been slain, Jarek had led them all in a mad charge up the Grand Stair, his swinging golden chain smashing anyone who resisted into pulp, whether they be flesh or shadow. Chosen and Spiritshadows alike had fled before him, and from Milla and all the Icecarls who came charging up behind her.

They had cleared the stairway in one frenzied charge and kept on going out into a large chamber. But there the charge had faltered. Chosen reinforcements poured in from the higher levels, including many Spiritshadows and guards who were accomplished at the more destructive light spells.

Attacked on three sides by a fusillade of Red Rays and other Light Magic, Milla had ordered a retreat, only to find her small force cut off from the Grand Stair by a large group of Chosen, who had used their superior knowledge of the Castle's many hidden ways to get behind the intruders. Unable to go down, Milla had led the way into the Underfolk corridors, a maze of smaller passages that allowed the Chosen's servants to move through the Castle without disturbing their masters.

But the Chosen had followed, and every turn Milla took it seemed they were there ahead of her. More and more Chosen and more Spiritshadows, steadily boxing them in. Milla had tried to break out through the weakest-looking bunch, but there were too many of them and they were too quickly reinforced. Milla alone with the Talon might have been able to fight her way through, but only at the cost of all her people.

"We'll stand here," answered Milla to Saylsen. *Here* was a large Underfolk storage chamber, a rough-hewn cavern easily two hundred stretches in diameter, with a very high ceiling. It had five doors of varying sizes, all of them now spiked shut by the Icecarls. Milla knew there were Chosen behind each exit. The doors wouldn't stop Spiritshadows, or hold the Chosen if they blasted through.

There was no choice but to make a stand.

"We will build a ship-fort here," Milla continued, indicating the barrels and full sacks that lined the walls. "We will hold it until the main host relieves us."

Saylsen nodded and immediately started to shout orders to the Icecarls. Milla counted them quickly as they ran to roll barrels together and build walls with the sacks. One sack spilled open, showering an Icecarl with an avalanche of shiny black seed-pods. It distracted Milla from her count for a second, but there were too few survivors for her to need to recount. Fourteen in total. Herself, Odris, Saylsen, Jarek, the Crone Malen, five Shield Maidens and four Icecarl hunters.

Malen was standing alone, completely still, her hands cupped to her temples. Milla knew she was trying to make contact with the other Crones. Young and relatively inexperienced, Malen had found she could not reach the strange group mind of the Crones unless she was calm and silent, the absolute opposite of being in a battle.

Being unable to communicate with the Crones via Malen meant that Milla had no idea where the main host was. They might still be on the Mountain of Light, or even now they could be advancing up through the Underfolk levels. Similarly, Milla didn't know how the rest of her advance guard was faring, spread out as it was through the Underfolk levels. In retrospect it had been a big mistake to go charging up the Grand Stair. Or at least to keep on charging after they had initially beaten the enemy away.

It was a mistake that Milla would probably pay for with her life, and the lives of everyone she led.

Malen dropped her hands, but even before she asked, Milla knew that the Crone had not been successful. It was evident in her face and defeated posture.

"News?"

Malen shook her head. There were tears in the corners of her eyes, not of sorrow, but of fierce concentration.

"I cannot still my thoughts," Malen said. "It is the first lesson of the Crones, but I have lost it… I had not thought I could."

She drew herself up and clapped her fists together before continuing.

"I have failed you, War-Chief," she said. "If we should survive this battle, I will ask leave to go to the Ice."

Milla frowned. Was this how she had seemed to the Crones herself? A proud young Icecarl demanding death upon the Ice rather than facing up to the problems that confronted her?

"That will not be necessary," Milla said sharply. "You have not failed me or any of us. Crones do not go to battle and I expect this is why. I am sure you will hear the Crones again. For now, I think we should both start shifting barrels. The Chosen will attack soon enough."

Malen clapped her fists together again, but Milla was not fooled. She knew that look. Malen *would* ask to go to the Ice. Well, that was a problem for later, Milla thought. There was only a small chance they would get out of here alive anyway. She turned her back on the Crone and went to help a pair of Shield Maidens wrestle a particularly large and sloshing barrel over to join their rapidly rising fort in the centre of the cavern.

Tal opened his eyes. The crystal globe was gone. He was lying on the floor somewhere and there was a voice droning on in the distance. Tal sat up and saw that he was in the Senior Lectorium, up on the last tier of the auditorium, between two desks. The Lectorium was empty, save for himself and the Lector, who was speaking from the central pulpit.

It was Lector Roum, Tal's chief teacher. A tall and solidly built Chosen, a Brightstar of the Blue, and so proud of it he dyed his beard blue and wore tiny Sunstones woven into it.

"Your father is missing, believed to be dead," Lector Roum suddenly roared, pointing his finger at Tal.

As the Lector's shout echoed through the Lectorium, his skin split apart like a fresh fruit, revealing a Spiritshadow within – a huge Spiritshadow, a formless mass of darkness that kept spilling out of the Lector's body. It was a black tide, unstoppable, implacable, flowing up the tiers, reaching hungrily for Tal.

He turned to flee, took one step and was suddenly stepping off one of the golden rods that suspended the Sunstone nets high above in the Red Tower. Stepping off into thin air.

Tal screamed and tried to grab something, his arms and legs flailing as he fell.

It was only then that he realised he was awake inside a dream. No, not a dream.

A nightmare.

Tal closed his eyes and the scream faded away. He still felt as if he were falling, and it was as cold as it had been when he really fell from the Red Tower. His shadowguard had saved him then. Perhaps that was what would happen in this nightmare.

Then he hit something. Tal opened his eyes to

find that he was not falling any more. He was floating in the reservoir beneath the Castle. The reservoir that was home to the water-spiders.

Desperately, Tal started swimming. But he didn't know what he was swimming towards. Unlike the real reservoir, this one was well lit, with an even white light that extended as far as he could see.

He couldn't see any water-spiders at first, but then in between two blinks of an eye, they were all around him. Huge, bulbous-bodied spiders scurrying across the surface of the water. Their multifaceted eyes were glowing like Sunstones. Venom dripped from their fangs.

If they killed him in a dream, would he die for real?

"It's only a dream!" Tal shouted in panic. "It's only a dream!"

The water-spiders scurried closer. They were bigger than the real ones. They grew as they approached, getting larger and larger, their fangs sharper and longer, dripping with more poison.

Desperately Tal tried to remember what Milla had done to survive the nightmare machine. She had practised her Rovkir breathing, he knew, a form of deep meditation. But he didn't know how to do that.

What he did know, he realised, was the deep concentration of Light Magic. Perhaps if he lost himself in that it would have the same effect.

Tal shut his eyes and concentrated. He felt inside himself for the deep, pure Violet of the Seventh and most important Keystone. He willed the light to fill his mind, to infuse his entire body. He used the Violet to force back all thoughts of water-spiders, one-eyed Merwin, Sushin, Sharrakor and other horrors that might be summoned into his dreams. Worst of all was that awful moment when he'd brought the ceiling down, killing Crow, Ebbitt and the others. He had to stop that nightmare somehow.

There was Violet. Only Violet. Nothing else existed.

Yet there was still one tiny part of his mind that kept screaming, one small remnant that screamed on and on, flinching with every second as it expected the stab of a spider's fangs, the pain of flowing poison...

But no stabbing pain came. Violet light filled Tal's body. He felt calm and secure. Soon even the slightest remaining fear was banished. He was Emperor, wielder of the Violet Keystone. He was in command.

Tal opened his eyes. There was a violet glow all around him, but beyond that there was nothing. He was floating in nothingness, in darkness. He could feel no breath of wind, no ground beneath him. He was somewhere beyond the reach of the nightmares, but beyond everything else as well.

For a moment, Tal almost panicked. But the violet glow fought against that. It lent him confidence, bathed him in self-assurance. He would find the way out. He must.

The Crones, thought Tal. The Crones had come to Milla and helped her out of the nightmare. Tal would have to call them.

But how? Unlike Milla he had not been trained to call the Crones into his nightmares. It was a skill all Icecarl children were taught, but Tal was a Chosen.

Tal did have one link with the Icecarls. He bared

his wrist, looking at the triangular scar there, the mark of his oath. The cuts had healed well, but were still very obvious, thin lines of raised scar tissue. Tal had thought the Crone crazy at the time, to cut him so dangerously. But he had grown used to the scars in time, and even to the idea that they linked him to Milla and the Clan of the Far-Raiders.

Tal rested two fingers across the scar. He tried to remember the feel of the bone ship's deck, the freezing wind, the humming of the rigging of the iceship, the clap of the sails. He cast his mind back to that time, to the Crone of the Far-Raiders who had made the cuts, to the Crone Mother who had spoken in prophecy. He tried to call them with a silent, mental shout.

Nothing happened. Still Tal persevered. He kept up his call and tried to remember all the small details from his time on the Ice with the Far-Raiders. The smell of the Selski soup. The exact colour of the Sunstone that was bound to the mast. The snort of the Wreska. The distant crash of Selski in their eternal pursuit of the Slepenish.

Slowly he felt the void around him change. Wind

came, a freezing wind. Then light, the particular colour of the Far-Raider's Sunstone. He felt bone planks beneath him, shuddering and shifting as the ship rode the Ice.

The darkness retreated. Tal stood next to the main mast of an Icecarl ship, in the pool of light from the Sunstone high above. The ship was under full sail, streaking across the Ice, a star shooting through the darkness.

There was someone else on the deck. Not a Crone, as Tal first thought. A Chosen. Fashnek. A whole Fashnek, his body repaired in this dream, without his Spiritshadow half.

He looked scared, raising his arms in horror as Tal stalked towards him, his violet glow forming a blinding nimbus around his head.

"Fashnek!" shouted Tal above the wind. "I am the Heir of Ramellan, Emperor of the Chosen, and you will be—"

Before he could say any more, Fashnek disappeared.

"Dark take it!" swore Tal. He had hoped he could force Fashnek to release him, since there was no sign of the Crones. It did seem as if he had defeated the nightmare machine, but that was not enough. Even if he could choose his own dreams, he was still a prisoner. And who knew what was going on back in the Castle? Even now, Sushin might be using Tal's half of the Violet Keystone to destroy the Veil.

The Icecarls had barely finished rolling the last of the barrels into their makeshift fort when the Sunstones in the ceiling high above flickered and then grew much brighter.

Milla was the first to realise that the stones were being manipulated from a distance. The only possible reason to brighten them would be to make Spiritshadows stronger. Obviously the Chosen were about to attack!

"Into the fort!" Milla shouted, waving in the few Icecarls who were still carrying sacks over from the walls.

Within a minute, Milla's small force was at the

ready, crammed into their tight circle of barrels and sacks. Milla looked at them, so out of place in this great stone room in their furs and bone face masks, made for a life out upon the Ice. She had led them badly, and not just them, but all Icecarls. The fate of their world had been put into her hands and she had failed.

"They come," hissed Saylsen.

Milla looked over the barrier. Spiritshadows were slithering in through every still-closed door, sliding along the floor before standing up along the walls. Spiritshadows of all kinds, from the thin-waisted humanoids of the guards to strange, insectlike things with multiple body parts and too many legs.

More and more Spiritshadows kept pouring in and lining up along the walls. At least a hundred Spiritshadows, and more flowing through every second, to join the massed ranks on all four sides of the Icecarls' fort. There was no sign of any Chosen trying to open the doors and follow them. Milla wondered if they were free shadows, the forerunners of an invasion force from Aenir.

"They are bound shadows, not free ones," said Odris. The Spiritshadow could often tell what Milla was thinking. "I expect some of them won't make it far from the doors, unless their masters follow. They'll snap back."

"I don't think it will make that much difference," muttered Milla.

"The Chosen mean to overwhelm us with shadows," Saylsen observed. "Cowards!"

No, not cowards, thought Milla. It was only common sense for the Chosen to save themselves as much as possible from injury and death. Besides, they had to know that apart from Milla's Talon and Jarek's golden chain, the Icecarls had few weapons to use against the Spiritshadows. Just one Merwin-horn sword and some glowing algae-coated spears. They had long since used all their shadowsacks and shadowbottles.

As the Spiritshadows flickered and moved into position, Milla ran through everything she could do, all the weapons or tactics they could employ.

"A Shield Maiden thinks of all things possible and expected, then does the impossible and unexpected."

She didn't realise she'd spoken aloud until Saylsen looked at her approvingly. At the same time, Milla realised there was one weapon she hadn't thought of using, one that was particularly effective against Spiritshadows when used properly.

Her Sunstone. The only problem was that she didn't really know how to use it. Tal had given her a few lessons, and she'd practised a little in the heatways on the way out, but that was all.

Milla stared down at the stone, watching the sparks of light inside it. What should she try and do? A Red Ray of Destruction? She'd seen enough of them. But hadn't Tal told her that Violet was the most powerful light of the spectrum? At this point, with the Spiritshadows outnumbering them twenty to one, surely it would be better to try a Violet Ray of Destruction.

Or better still, a Violet *Wave* of Destruction.

"Milla? What are you doing?" asked Odris nervously as Milla raised her hand and bent her head to focus on the Sunstone.

Milla ignored her. The flow of Spiritshadows

through the doors was lessening and their ranks were almost complete. They would attack very soon, unless she did something.

Focus, concentration and visualisation – that was what Tal had said. Milla bent her mind upon the Sunstone, shutting out everything else. It was rather like the second stage of Rovkir breathing, Milla thought, and was surprised to find that she'd actually started the breathing pattern.

Violet. Violet. Milla willed the Sunstone to produce Violet. She needed to make a great pool of Violet inside the stone and then unleash it like an avalanche upon the Spiritshadows. Even if it only took out the ranks in front of her, that would give them a chance.

Milla remembered a real avalanche she had seen once. It was at a gathering between the Far-Raiders and their sister clan, the Frostfighters. Both clans had left their ships under skeleton crews to celebrate and feast upon the lesser peak of Twoknuckle Mountain. It had been a great but risky celebration as the mountain was known to be dangerous. It was sheer bravado that had led the clans to choose it. Even so, the Crones had insisted on some precaution being taken and hundreds of moth lanterns were laid in expanding rings around the central fires.

Halfway through the feast, the higher peak of Twoknuckle shrugged, sending down a vast wave of snow and ice. They had heard it first, a deep roar in the darkness, louder than any beast. The outer ring of lanterns was snuffed out in an instant and for a few blinks the inner ring lit up the avalanche as it fell upon the camp. Milla remembered it well, a wall of icy death that swept away everyone who wasn't quick enough to find shelter behind the clusters of rock.

It was an avalanche she imagined now, one of solid Violet. She called it up out of the stone, using all the powers of concentration and all the discipline that made her such a dangerous fighter.

Violet flared. Icecarls gasped. Odris stepped even further away and said something that Milla was too focused to hear. She could feel the avalanche coming, could feel the Violet power rising in the stone. Her hand was shaking, her whole body trembling, as if a real avalanche was roaring down upon her.

Instinct told her when to thrust her hand forward and let the power go – at exactly the same moment the Spiritshadows charged.

Milla shouted a war cry as Violet light leaped from her Sunstone and spread into a wave. It was as wide as the fort and tall as an Icecarl, rushing forward with a deafening crash and rumble. The wave swept every Spiritshadow before it, sending them crashing and tumbling back through the walls and doors.

The Icecarls cheered, but only briefly. One attack had been forestalled. There were still three forces coming from the remaining sides.

"Sell your lives dearly!" Milla shouted as she dashed towards the side the Spiritshadows would reach first. She was surprised to find Odris speeding ahead of her, and on the side she wore the Talon. Nothing had ever made Odris come that close before.

"It's coming back!" Odris warned. "Look out!"

Milla looked behind her. The Violet wave had

rebounded from the wall and was ricocheting towards them. It looked stronger and more menacing from this side and showed no signs of weakening. It had veered a little to one side in the rebound. Only half of it would strike the Icecarls' fort.

"To this side!" Saylsen cried, her voice at full roar in an effort to be heard above the rumble of the wave. "To this side!"

Everyone was running to the safer side when the Violet wave hit. Milla watched aghast as it picked up huge barrels and hurled them towards the ceiling. Sacks were blown apart. One of the Shield Maidens, already wounded and slow, was lifted up, thrown down on to the floor and then rocketed out the back of the wave. If two of her companions hadn't caught her, she would have broken her neck.

Still the wave of light kept going. Spiritshadows, attacking only a moment before, fled in all directions as the Icecarls hunkered down as best they could, shielding themselves from the spray of debris.

"Well done!" shouted Saylsen to Milla. "The

enemy flees! Let it run one more time through, then stop it!"

"Stop it?" Milla yelled back. "I don't even know how I started it!"

Tal had just about given up on the Crones and any hope of escaping from his dream when he spotted a black-clad figure approaching across the Ice. A Crone, skating without skates, moving as fast as the iceship, though it was under full sail. Tal had tried to slow the ship down, but had only succeeded in changing the colour of the Sunstone on the mast. Apparently he had to know how something worked in order to dream it properly. Or else thinking he had to know something stopped him from dreaming it. He could go mad thinking in circles like that.

Tal glanced away for a moment. When he looked

back the Crone was suddenly there, standing next to him. He jumped, then he realised it was the Crone of the Far-Raiders, the first Crone he had ever met.

She smiled at him, her silver eyes twinkling, but she didn't speak.

"Please feel free to talk," said Tal. "It's my dream after all."

The Crone smiled again, but remained silent. She seemed to be waiting.

"Am I supposed to do something?" asked Tal politely. He couldn't quite remember what Milla said happened when the Crones showed up. Except maybe this wasn't truly a Crone. Maybe he'd just dreamed up a Crone, instead of having a real Crone entering his dreams, so she couldn't actually help…

"Stop it!" muttered Tal to himself.

"Stop what?" asked a familiar voice.

Tal whirled around. Adras was floating behind him, but in his Aeniran Storm Shepherd form, not as a Spiritshadow. Which was impossible. All Aenirans turned into Spiritshadows in the Dark World.

"Where are we?" asked Adras, scratching his

cloudy head with one puffy finger.

"In my dream," said Tal. "Are you you, or are you me dreaming you?"

"What?" asked Adras. "The last thing I remember is falling asleep."

"Yes, but I could easily dream you saying that," said Tal. "Oh, who cares! Hopefully we'll wake up soon."

He turned back to the Crone and jumped again. The deck was crowded with Crones now. Lots of Crones, and a Crone Mother sitting there in a high-backed chair of bone.

"Who are they?" Adras asked as he puffed himself up to full size. Lightning crackled in his fists. "Are they enemies?"

"No!" said Tal hastily. "They're Icecarls. Like Milla."

"They're a lot uglier than Milla," remarked Adras, but he let the lightning crackle away into the air.

The Crones slid forward. Tal watched them nervously, but didn't move as they clustered all around him. He had to shut his eyes, unable to meet their stares.

He felt the Crones pick him up and opened his eyes again. He saw the mast and its Sunstone high above, and the darkness beyond.

The Crones threw him up in the air. It was exhilarating to be thrown and caught again. The first time he went up half as high as the mast. The second time he was level with the Sunstone at the very top.

The third time he didn't come back down. He just kept going up and up and up into the dark sky. Then there was a tremendous flash of light and all of a sudden Tal was wide awake, crouched inside the crystal globe. Fashnek was only a few stretches away, frantically turning the wheel that controlled the green gas. Vapours were beginning to swirl around Tal's feet again, but he ignored them.

Without hesitation, he reached out to the seven Sunstones around him and took control. Each one flashed, then steadied into the appropriate colour – the code to unlock the crystal globe.

There was a faint click and the globe split at its equator. Tal threw it fully open and jumped out. Fashnek shrieked, a strangely high-pitched shriek for a Chosen. He dropped the Sunstone he held in his right hand and scuttled back, both of his halves in total panic.

Tal snatched up the Sunstone as it skittered across the floor.

"No, no, it wasn't me," moaned Fashnek in one breath, and then in the other, "Get him! Kill him!"

His two Spiritshadow companions obeyed. The Urglegurgle bounced twice and launched itself at Tal's head, while the wasp-waisted shadow lunged forward to grab his legs.

Once again Tal acted instinctively, almost without thought. He stepped back against the globe. Still in tune with the seven Sunstones, he summoned a thin line of Violet from each of them, to form a fence of light around himself.

The Urglegurgle hit the fence as it came down and was split in two as cleanly as a cut apple. Each half landed badly and bounced away. They came together for a moment, failed to join, and then there was a *pop* as the Urglegurgle disappeared, either back to Aenir or destroyed for good.

The thin-waisted Spiritshadow was quicker. It

twisted away, losing only a hand to the Violet wire.

Tal raised the Sunstone he had picked up off the floor. The Spiritshadow raised its remaining hand in a gesture of defeat and vanished. Its rapid disappearance troubled Tal. It showed that free Spiritshadows could retreat to Aenir whenever they wanted to. He hoped it was much harder for them to come back, though with the Veil weakened and possibly already failing, it might not be.

"Spare me, noble master," whined Fashnek, prostrating himself on the floor. "I am but a humble servant of the Empress."

"The Empress is dead," Tal said harshly. "Besides, I know your true master is Sushin. Where is my Spiritshadow?"

"A deal, an agreement, your Spiritshadow for my miserable life," Fashnek whimpered. "Oh, your generosity—"

Tal held his Sunstone high. Red light flared, bathing Fashnek in its glow, making the sweat on his face look like beads of blood.

"In the shadowbottle over there!"

Tal looked where Fashnek pointed. There was a

bottle of golden metal on one of the worktables. But there were other bottles and containers strewn around the room.

"You open it," Tal instructed. "And I might let you live."

"Yes, of course, great lord," Fashnek replied. He slowly levered himself up and hobbled towards the table. Tal kept his distance, the Sunstone ready.

"You will be Emperor, I am sure," mumbled Fashnek as he struggled with the stopper on the bottle. "I saw the Violet in you. I know these things. And an Emperor always needs a Master of Nightmares, no? I will serve you as I served Her Majesty. Sushin, why, he is nothing, a nobody—"

"Shut up!" ordered Tal. "If I am ever Emperor, there will be no Hall of Nightmares at all!"

"So you say now, Master, so you say... ah!"

With a last heave from his good hand, the stopper came free. A shadow erupted forth, a great stream of roaring darkness that rapidly assumed the familiar shape of Adras. A very angry Adras, shadow-lightning flickering not just from his hands, but also from his eyes.

"Jailer, die!"

With that, Adras grabbed the shadow-half of Fashnek around its insectoid head and began to twist, shadow-lightning flickering all around and thunder rumbling.

Fashnek screamed. Tal started forward, shouting, "No!"

But it was too late. Adras bellowed in triumph as the Spiritshadow's head came off. He threw it on the ground and trampled on it, letting Fashnek's body fall to the floor.

"No one will lock Adras in a tiny bottle ever again!"

Tal knelt down next to Fashnek. The Master of Nightmares stared up at him, his eyes glassy with shock. The shadow-half that had sustained him was already fading into nothingness. Where it had been, there was no skin and Tal could see bone and internal organs, even though he tried not to look.

"It was a mistake," whispered Fashnek. "A terrible mistake. I was afraid of dying... yet there are things worse than death... It was Sharrakor who wounded me, in dragon-shape, and Sharrakor who gave me life. I should not have taken it from his hands. But perhaps it has all been only a nightmare, all in my dream machines..."

"No," said Tal, thinking of Bennem and Crow's parents and Jarnil, and all the people who had been tormented by Fashnek and his machines, many of them to their deaths. "*You* were the nightmare."

But Fashnek didn't hear him. He was already dead.

There were no Spiritshadows left in the cavern, which was good, thought Milla. But there was nothing left of the makeshift fort either, and her little band of Icecarls was tiring rapidly as they dashed from side to side in their efforts to avoid the Violet wave. It hadn't lessened in size or power at all, though it was becoming more erratic in direction and harder to predict every time it rebounded from a wall.

"Left!" shouted Saylsen, and they all ran left, until the Shield Mother shouted, "Stop!" and then, "Dark take it! Right a bit!"

The Violet wave missed them by a few stretches,

hurtling past towards the far wall. It would be a few minutes before it came sweeping back in at a new angle.

"Have you tried reversing whatever it was you did?" asked Malen. She didn't look at Milla. Like everyone else she kept her eyes on the wave.

"No," snapped Milla. Every time she started to focus on the Sunstone, the Violet wave would come back. Someone would grab her and drag her out of the way, and her concentration would be gone. Besides, all she could think of was the avalanche. Trying *not* to think of an avalanche only made the image even stronger in her head. So even if she could concentrate on her Sunstone, it was likely she would just create another Violet wave. Two would kill everyone for certain.

"We'll have to try one of the doors again," Saylsen said grimly. "We can't run away from this thing forever."

"Odris! Have a look and see what's behind that one," ordered Milla, pointing to one of the doors. There were only two exits left to try out of the five. One stone door and part of the corridor behind it had been totally smashed by the wave and was now impassable. Two others were so heavily barricaded and defended that there was no chance of getting through.

"I'll get my head pulled off if I poke it through," Odris protested. "*You* have a look if you want!"

"*I* can't stick my head through a closed door," said Milla. "You can. Would you prefer to get swept up by the wave?"

"*I'm* not tired," said Odris mulishly. "I can keep away from—"

"Left!" shouted Saylsen. "Left!"

Odris was the only one who hadn't been watching the wave. As Saylsen shouted, she moved right instead of left.

"This way!" yelled Milla. "*This* way!"

The wave rushed on. Odris, caught in front of it, didn't follow Milla. Instead she ran in front of the wave, before launching herself into the air and hurling herself at the door Milla had indicated. A second after she went through it, the wave hit with a deafening crash. Once again, it rebounded to groans from all the Icecarls.

"Surely it has to stop soon," puffed Malen. "I did not think Sunstones were so strong."

"Neither did I," muttered Milla. All the Light Magic she had seen before had only lasted as long as the caster concentrated on it. This thing she had created seemed to have a life of its own. Milla anxiously looked at the door Odris had gone through. She could feel the Spiritshadow's absence – a sort of dull ache that was hard to pin down, rather like a toothache. But at least there was no worse feeling. If Odris was being hurt by other Spiritshadows, Milla would feel some of her pain.

"Head for the door," Milla ordered after a quick look to make sure they would still be able to avoid the wave's return passage. "Odris isn't fighting, so maybe we can get through."

They were halfway over to it when the door opened. But instead of Odris, there was a Chosen woman, a Sunstone in her hand and an unfamiliar Spiritshadow at her back, a huge bird-thing with eyebrows like horns.

Milla opened her mouth to order a sudden charge, but snapped it shut as another Chosen emerged behind the woman. This time it was someone she knew. Tal's eccentric great-uncle Ebbitt, now clad in a weird assortment of crystal armour plates in many different, shining colours. To top it all off, he was wearing a golden metal saucepan on his head, cushioned by a scarf of bright indigo.

Milla couldn't help smiling. From their very first meeting when Tal had taken her to his great-uncle's lair, she had liked Ebbitt. That meeting seemed very long ago. Now Tal was who knew where, she was surrounded... but just the sight of Ebbitt brought sudden hope.

"Quick! Quick!" Ebbitt called out. "This is an escape in progress!"

The Icecarls needed no urging. The wave was already rushing down upon them. Despite their weariness, they started to run for the door, which was wide enough for three people to pass through at one time.

"What is that?!" exclaimed Ebbitt as he saw the wave. The woman with him exclaimed something too, then both of them raised their Sunstones as one and twin beams of intense white light shot out to meet the wave.

As the White Rays hit, the wave faltered and slowed. But it did not stop fully, nor disappear, as the two Chosen seemed to expect.

"Too strong!" gasped the woman. "I cannot hold it!"

Her light snapped off and she fell back to be caught in the gentle claws of her Spiritshadow.

Ebbitt kept up his White Ray, but the wave began to speed up again. Ebbitt started to back up, passing through the doorway with the last of the Icecarls, the Wilder Jarek, who was still in his post-fury state. He could move and fight quickly enough, but would not speak and his eyes remained strange and distant.

"Get... ready to... slam door," instructed Ebbitt. Sweat was pouring off his face as if he were physically holding back a great weight. His Sunstone was so bright that Milla could not look at it, and the White Ray was equally blinding.

"Now!" shouted Ebbitt, and the White Ray disappeared.

Milla and Saylsen hurled the door shut and stepped back, just as the wave hit the other side.

7

Stone screeched and the door shuddered. For a terrible moment Milla thought it was going to explode inward, but then it stilled. The wave had rebounded again.

"Quick, quicker, quickest!" said Ebbitt as he dashed down the line of Icecarls. "We must away!"

He led them down a corridor, past four dead or unconscious Chosen, to a T-junction where Odris was busy prying loose stones out of the end of the corridor and piling them against a door.

Ebbitt went to the seemingly solid wall opposite the door and pressed carefully in several places. Nothing happened. He looked puzzled for a moment, then pressed in entirely different places. He was answered by a deep rumble under the floor. The wall pivoted in place to reveal a narrow entry and a flight of steps leading down.

"The out-way. Go help Odris!" cried Ebbitt, going over to pry out a stone himself from where Odris had begun to demolish the wall. The stone was bigger than he expected, came out suddenly and fell on the floor, narrowly missing his feet.

As the stone rolled to a stop, a spot of blue light suddenly appeared on the door, smoke curling up from it. The light began to fizz and spit wood chips, steadily cutting through and down the door. Someone was breaking in from the other side.

"More stones!" boomed Odris. The Icecarls rushed to help her, forming a chain to pass on the stones that the stronger Spiritshadow pulled out of the wall.

In a few minutes, the door was buried beneath a cairn of stones. Blue light still flashed up through the gaps, but even after the Chosen cut through the door, the piled-up stones would delay them for a little while.

"Down with the established order," said Ebbitt. "Hurry! I shall shut the gate."

Though Saylsen tried to get in front of her, Milla led the way down the steps. Not because she didn't trust Ebbitt, but if it was some sort of trap, she at least had the Talon to deal with it.

The stair led down to a very damp, wet room with walls that wept beads of water. Algae was slowly dying all around, making it clear that the whole place had been submerged until very recently.

Milla heard the wall grind shut above them as the last of her Icecarls entered the room. Shortly after, Ebbitt appeared. He pressed several stones on the floor in a particular combination, which made a section of the wall slide across to block the stairway behind them.

"There's another way out, isn't there?" asked Milla as Ebbitt took off his saucepan helmet and wiped his brow with a patchwork handkerchief that he pulled out from under his shoulder plate.

"Out? Out? We've only just got here," replied Ebbitt. "*Of course* there is another way out. We'll have to hope that no one else knows how to control the surge system though."

Milla looked around at the algae and the dripping water and sighed. It was good to have got away from the Violet wave and the Chosen, but she was still cut off from the rest of her forces. She felt the frustration of it deep inside every muscle. She wanted to run and shout and attack the enemy, but that was not wise.

"Malen, see if you can reach the Crones," she ordered. "We will rest here for a little while.

"We thank you for your rescue," Milla said formally to Ebbitt and the Chosen woman.

"I haven't seen anything like that wave since Mercur's day," said Ebbitt thoughtfully.

"Then you've never seen anything like it, because you aren't that old, Uncle," said the woman. With the help of her Spiritshadow, she stood up and looked at the assembled Icecarls. Her eyes fell on Saylsen. "Are you Milla?"

Milla looked back and drew herself up on her toes a bit. The Chosen woman was quite a bit taller. She looked much more shaken by her efforts to control the Violet wave than Ebbitt. Her skin was very pale and her Spiritshadow was surreptitiously helping her stand up.

"I am Saylsen, Shield Mother. That is Milla Talon-Hand, War-Chief of the Icecarls," pronounced Saylsen as she pointed at Milla. "Who are you?"

"I am Graile Parel-Kessil," answered the Chosen. She seemed a bit surprised by Milla's age and Saylsen's announcement. "Tal's mother."

"Tal's mother!" exclaimed Milla. "But he said you were sick, likely to die."

"I was poisoned," said Graile. "Tal brought me the antidote."

"Tal is here?" asked Milla. "That is good. Why is he not with you?"

"He was captured when he came to me," Graile explained. "Ebbitt says he has been taken to the Hall of Nightmares. The Codex told him."

Milla frowned. Her first priority was to rejoin her forces and find out where the main host was. But Tal in the Hall of Nightmares? For all his failings, she did not want him to be killed, or end up like Bennem, wandering inside his own head forever.

"Tal must be rescued, though I cannot see yet how it can be done," pronounced Milla.

"Ebbitt told me that—" Graile said.

"When did you speak to the Codex?" interrupted Malen.

"Er, quite recently. The Codex also told me that Sushin has Tal's Sunstone," said Ebbitt. For once his voice didn't quaver and he didn't sound half-crazy, though his fingers were beating on his crystal breastplate in a nervous way. "Half of the Violet Keystone, the Codex said. I didn't believe the thing, for I had split that stone myself. But then I saw the Violet wave and I am guessing that was your work, Milla Thingummy-Hand. So maybe it is true."

"I did make the wave," said Milla.

"May I see your Sunstone?" asked Ebbitt.

Silently, Milla raised her hand to show her ring. Her Sunstone shone there as usual, a deep yellow shot through with red sparks. Ebbitt raised his own Sunstone and shone a thin ray of Violet at Milla's stone. The ray hit and Milla's Sunstone exploded into vibrant Violet light, flooding the whole room with its brilliance.

"It *is* the Violet Keystone!" exclaimed Graile. "Or part of it."

"Hmmpff," said Ebbitt. He seemed annoyed that he hadn't realised it before. Then he slowly and creakily sank down on to one knee, his crystal armour clanking. "I suppose this makes you Empress or something."

"No, it is Tal who should be Emperor when the time comes," said Graile swiftly. "The candidate must be ratified by the Assembly, and Tal is a Chosen and also bears a Violet Keystone."

"Not if Sushin's stolen it," Ebbitt grumbled. "I rather like the idea of an Icecarl Empress. Of course, we'll have to get rid of the old one."

Graile flinched as Ebbitt spoke this treason and looked away.

Milla stared down at the old man. She was tired and, though she would not admit it, slightly in shock from the fighting they had been through. What were they going on about?

"Because I have the Violet Keystone I am the

Chosen Empress?" she asked. "But doesn't that mean that if Sushin has the other half now the Chosen will say he is the Emperor? And Tal must be rescued whether he's Emperor or not."

"Oh, Crow's gone off to rescue Tal," said Ebbitt airily, waving his hand around as if it suddenly had a life of its own. "And since Sushin is going off to destroy the Veil with his half of the Violet Keystone, it is hardly likely anyone will want to call him Emperor."

Milla shook her head. She felt like she wasn't hearing properly. Crow and Tal were practically sworn enemies.

"You've sent *Crow* to rescue Tal? And who is going to stop Sushin from destroying the Veil?"

Ebbitt stopped waving. He pulled his arm back and bent his hand as if he were imitating a bird for children, moving his thumb and fingers like a beak. Then his hand-puppet spoke, with Ebbitt throwing and changing his voice so realistically that the Icecarls jumped.

"Crow feels bad about Tal, so he will do his best to save him. I think he will succeed. Who will stop

Sushin? Why, Milla, of course! And Ebbitt and all the little Icecarls will help."

"Should we kill him?" asked Saylsen, frowning. This sort of madness could be contagious.

"No," sighed Milla. "I fear that he is speaking the truth. We will have to stop Sushin. Only I don't know how, or even where we should go to find him."

"The Seventh Tower," said Ebbitt, dropping his hand and speaking in his normal voice. "The Violet Tower. Everything will come together there, for better... or worse."

Tal looked down at the pathetic remnant that had been Fashnek. Adras stood next to him, still rumbling with distant thunder.

"'It was Sharrakor who wounded me, in dragon-shape, and Sharrakor who gave me life. I should not have taken it from his hands,'" Tal said quietly, repeating Fashnek's last words. "What in Light's name does that mean? How can a dragon have hands?"

"Jailer die," said Adras, which wasn't much help. "Where do we go now?"

Tal considered for a moment, biting his lip in anxiety. There was no point in looking for the

Underfolk, not since he'd accidentally killed Crow, Ebbitt and the others. But perhaps he could join the Icecarls who were attacking the Castle. Adras had sensed that Odris was with them, so Milla must be there too. At least Tal fervently hoped so. Otherwise she would have gone to the Ice and that would be another death on his conscience.

But Tal knew he couldn't just go and join the Icecarls. There was Sushin, always the enemy. Tal had to admit there was very little chance his mother had taken the stone before he passed out. Sushin almost certainly had Tal's half of the Violet Keystone, so he finally had the ability to destroy the Veil.

"I guess we have to go up," Tal said slowly. "Up to the Violet Tower. The Icecarls won't know what Sushin can do, at least not until it's too late. Even if Milla suspects Sushin, she won't know how to stop him."

"Sushin is the one who throws poison?" asked Adras. He puffed himself into a ball that was a reasonable imitation of Shadowmaster Sushin.

"Yes."

"I don't want to go there," said Adras. "I want to go to Odris."

"We have to go to the Violet Tower," repeated Tal. The more he thought about it, the more the urgency grew inside him. Sushin could be using the Violet Keystone right now as they wasted time talking. They had to get to the Violet Tower and stop him from destroying the Veil.

"I'm not going," announced Adras, folding his arms. "You can't make me."

Tal was about to let his anger burst out into words when they both heard someone open the door. Instantly Tal ducked behind one of the workbenches, and Adras shot up to the ceiling and spread himself out among the shadows there.

The unknown intruder was trying to be very quiet. The door only opened a little way and Tal saw someone slide in. In the dim light he couldn't even tell whether it was a Spiritshadow or someone wearing black.

Adras drifted over, ready to drop on the intruder. Tal lifted his Sunstone and it began to swirl with red light in preparation for a Ray of Destruction.

It was a person, Tal saw, not a Spiritshadow. All dressed in black, with a black hood drawn tightly around his face. Tal saw a dagger in the hand held close by the intruder's side. He moved from shadow to shadow, until he could see the open globe and the body of Fashnek. He stopped suddenly then and looked around.

"Tal?"

It was a voice from the past, a voice from the dead. Crow's voice.

But that was impossible. For a moment, Tal thought he might still be under the control of the nightmare machine. But the Sunstones on their silver stands were dark, the globe still open.

"Tal?"

Tal stood up slowly. Crow faced him and slowly undid his hood. He was very pale and there was a partly healed scar across his forehead.

"I thought I killed you," whispered Tal.

"Ebbitt saved us," said Crow.

"Ebbitt's alive too?" exclaimed Tal. He felt relief flood his entire body, making him feel weak. He needed to sit down.

"We all survived," said Crow. "I thought I'd killed *you*. And I did hit you on the head. I... I'm sorry. I guess I went crazy... There is so much the Chosen have done to my family..."

"I've been in the nightmare machine," said Tal. He didn't need to say anything else.

Crow nodded and went over to look down on Fashnek's body.

"It took too long to come to this," he said.

"I'm sorry too," said Tal after a moment. "For bringing down the roof. For everything my people have done to yours."

"It's all changing now," said Crow. "The Icecarls will win. They have agreed that we will be free."

"I hope that happens," replied Tal. He was surprised to find that he meant it. He had come to learn that there was no such thing as the natural superiority of the Chosen over everyone else. In fact, Tal realised with surprise that there were more Underfolk and Icecarls who he admired and looked up to.

"I came to rescue you," said Crow. "The Codex told Ebbitt where you were. Or so he said. Only you seem to have rescued yourself."

Silence fell awkwardly between them then. Tal still wasn't absolutely sure Crow could be trusted. Too much had happened between them in the past. Could the Freefolk boy have changed so much?

"Um, I have to go," Tal said after a few more seconds of uncomfortable silence.

"Where?" asked Crow.

"The Violet Tower," Tal answered slowly. "Sushin has part of the Violet Keystone. It's probably enough for him to destroy the Veil. The Sun will come again and melt the Ice. There will be an invasion of shadows. Thousands and thousands of shadows. I have to… I *have* to stop him."

"You will need help," said Crow.

"Like you helped me in the Red Tower?" asked Tal.

Crow shook his head.

"No. I swear it in my parents' names. We fight together now."

He clapped his fists, Icecarl-style, then drew out a Sunstone. For a moment Tal almost shot a Red Ray at him, but he forced himself to wait. Crow simply gave light in respect and Tal let out the breath he didn't know he'd held.

"All right," Tal agreed. He clapped his fists too and let the red light fade from his Sunstone in order to give light in return. It was Violet that shone forth, though he had not tried to make it so. Perhaps even without the Violet Keystone something of the imperial majesty clung to him.

"We'll fight together."

"Adras fight too," boomed the Spiritshadow from the ceiling. "Only can we fight someone easier, not Sushin?"

Tal ignored him.

"You said Ebbitt told you where I was? He didn't get hurt too much?"

"No. He was hurt, but he's all right now."

"And Milla is with the Icecarls?"

Crow laughed for a moment, then grew suddenly serious again.

"Milla is the *leader* of the Icecarls! She has a magical fingernail of crystal and Sunstone chips they call the Talon of Danir, and she is called Milla Talon-Hand, War-Chief of the Icecarls and Living

Sword of Asteyr. She has grown, I think – if not in size, in something… something you can't see. You have grown, too, Tal."

"What do you mean?" asked Tal. He looked down at himself. He didn't seem any taller or stronger or anything.

"You seem… more important," Crow said hesitantly, as if he wasn't sure himself. "Less a boy, and less a Chosen. You have become something else, something more."

"You have changed too, at least in your choice of colour," Tal said with a slight laugh. He wasn't sure he liked Crow being strange and mystical any more than he had liked him being aggressive and antagonistic.

Crow looked down at his black robes, so different from the white normally worn by Freefolk, or the white with black lettering of the Underfolk.

"It's true I've changed," he said. "Deeper than my clothes. I know what's really important now."

Tal tried to smile again, but found he couldn't.

"I'm glad Milla leads the Icecarls," he said. "She knows about the danger from Sushin. How far have the Icecarls penetrated into the Castle? And where is the current fighting? I know a few ways to get to the Violet levels, but they may be blocked off or defended."

Crow nodded. "Come, let's talk as we go. There is no fighting close by, at least not yet. There are also Underfolk ways to the Violet levels. I will show you. Follow me."

"I have to find out what is happening with the main force before we can go anywhere," Milla said sternly. She looked across at Malen, who was once more standing still in absolute concentration.

Ebbitt looked at the Crone and wiggled his eyebrows, trying to distract her. But Malen did not see him, though her pure blue eyes were open.

"There are many of your people in the lower Red levels," said Graile. She was lying down, exhausted, supported by both her own and Ebbitt's Spiritshadows. "At least, that is what I overheard a Chosen saying. Thousands of them, he said. I am still not entirely sure why you are invading our

Castle. But Uncle Ebbitt says we need you to stop Sushin from destroying the Veil, and I find myself believing him, which is not always the case. And my son sent me to you, not to any Chosen."

"Thousands?" asked Milla. "The main host must have arrived!"

Saylsen shook her head. "The Chosen may simply be afraid. Remember, 'In fear, nothing is certain. A single sharik becomes a swarm. Only the calm Shield Maiden can count.'"

Malen's eyes clouded. There was an instant hush. All the Icecarls leaned forward as if they too might hear what Malen heard.

"There is a Crone at the exit from the heatways below. She will come no further. She says that she has counted two thousand of our folk through and still they pass. Some wounded have come back, they say... They say we are victorious in the Red levels and the Chosen retreat upward into Orange!"

"Ask her to tell a Shield Mother that Milla Talon-Hand lives," instructed Milla. "That I must now fight my way to the Violet Tower. Tell her that the most senior Shield Mother should assume command and that they must keep attacking up through the levels, and try to join us in the Violet Tower as soon as they can."

"Feyle One-Ear will command if she still lives," said Saylsen. "We should send her a messenger as well, to be sure."

Milla looked around the green and dripping walls of the room.

"How do we get out of here?" she asked Ebbitt. "And how do we get to the Violet Tower?"

"It is a secret, but some can go by steam to the topmost Violet level," whispered Ebbitt, holding his finger upright next to his nose. "But first we must all jump in the bucket."

He pointed at the wall opposite the stairway they'd come down. There was no sign of any bucket, or a hidden door or stairway, but the Icecarls moved apart so Ebbitt could press his palms against various stones in a complicated sequence.

Nothing happened. Ebbitt scratched his head. Then he pressed his ear against the wall. Whatever he heard satisfied him and he stepped back.

Everyone waited for another minute, watching

the wall, before Odris spoke to Milla in her Storm Shepherd whisper, which could probably be heard through the wall as well as by all the Icecarls and Graile.

"Is something supposed to happen?"

"Yes," said Milla.

As she spoke, she felt a rumbling underfoot. All the Icecarls shifted nervously. It felt like breaking ice and their instinctive reaction was to run away from it as fast as possible.

"Um," said Ebbitt. "Perhaps it was the floor—"

He jumped back as the floor suddenly slid away under his feet, revealing a deep hole. Two Shield Maidens caught him and rushed him back still further, joining the general dash to the other wall.

When the rumbling stopped, almost a third of the floor had slid away, revealing a ramp that led down into a dark and stagnant pool of water.

"Damp," said Ebbitt. He started down the ramp, his Spiritshadow easing out from behind Graile to glide along at his heels. The old man paused at the edge of the water, pulled his breastplate away and spoke down, apparently to his own chest. "I advise you to hold your breath through here."

Before anyone could ask him what he was doing, his Sunstone shone brightly and a globe of green light formed around his head. His Spiritshadow went first, then the old man followed it confidently further down the ramp. Both of them disappeared underwater.

"Oh, Ebbitt," sighed Graile. "There's probably a perfectly easy and dry way out of here, but he has to choose the dirtiest and most difficult."

She started to get up, but even with her Spiritshadow's help she would have fallen if Milla had not caught her elbow.

"Thank you," gasped Graile. "I am still... very weak. Perhaps you could help me with a globe of air?"

"That is what Ebbitt made just then?" asked Milla. "To breathe under the water?"

"Yes. It is Green magic, not difficult. Air is compressed into the light. I don't think I could hold my breath at all, so I will need it."

"How do I begin?" asked Milla tentatively. She remembered the Violet wave all too well. What if she made a mistake and formed a globe around Graile's head that had no air in it?

"I will show you with my Sunstone," whispered Graile. "You need only follow what I do, but with more power. You regulate power with will – it is a matter of how fiercely you think it. I am sure you can do that."

Milla nodded. But before Graile could begin, Saylsen interrupted. All the Icecarls had been suspicious of Sunstone magic in the first place. Milla had only made it worse with the Violet wave. It made her feel strange deep inside to know that not only did she have the ability to use Sunstone magic, but that the Icecarls feared her for it.

"We should send someone through the water to take a look," the Shield Mother said. "To see that there is air on the other side, and that the way is clear."

"Odris can go," said Milla.

"The shadow does not breathe," said Saylsen. "We need to know that we can make it through without magic."

"Milla could make you each a globe of air," said

Graile weakly. "It would not take long."

Milla saw the resistance on every Icecarl face, but no one spoke. If she ordered it, they would accept. But she would not order them, and once again she felt a pang in her heart as she was reminded how distant she now was from the Shield Maidens and hunters who stood before her.

"Send who you will," Milla said. "But tie a cord to them first, in case of trouble." She turned back to Graile. "Show me," said Milla. "I will make a globe of air for you, but we will cross the water without magic. That is the Icecarl way."

10

After three attempts to cross one of the major colourless corridors to get to an essential stairway, Tal was forced to accept that he would have to ask Crow to show him an Underfolk way to the Violet levels. Every time they were about to run across, large groups of armed Chosen, usually led by a guard, would appear at one end of the corridor, hurrying along. It was clear that the entire adult population of Chosen, including some older children, was being mobilised against the Icecarl invasion.

Many of them would be killed or injured, Tal thought sadly, all of them fighting for a lie. They were not defending themselves, but were simply dupes of Sushin and Sharrakor. The Aeniran plan to destroy the Veil and take over the Dark World had long been in action. Even the Empress had been controlled by Sharrakor.

"Go, don't go, back, stop," grumbled Adras. "This is a silly game."

"It's not a game, Adras," said Tal. "Crow, do you know a way we can get up through Orange and Yellow?"

"I know a way to get right up to Violet One," said Crow with a slight smile. "But it's not pleasant or easy.

"Tal didn't like the look of that smile. It reminded him of the old Crow, the one who had hit him on the head and stolen his Sunstone.

"What is it, then?"

The smile disappeared and Crow grew more serious. "You know the laundry chute?"

Tal nodded. Everyone knew the laundry chute. But you couldn't climb it – it was made to slide down. Besides, he'd used it to escape from Sushin before. It was sure to be guarded.

"There is another, similar chute," said Crow. "Except that it's a vertical shaft, without any turns. It runs from the Underfolk serving kitchen on Violet One all the way down – down to the heatways or even lower. It's called the slopdown."

"The slopdown?" asked Tal. That didn't sound too good.

Crow saw the look on Tal's face and nodded. "It's for the kitchen waste from each level. So it smells bad and it's pretty slimy. But there is a metal ladder that goes all the way. I think."

"You've climbed it?" asked Tal.

"Only as far as Indigo Seven," said Crow. "That's why I don't know whether the ladder goes the whole way. But you can get out at any kitchen on any level. The main danger is the slipperiness, or hot slops."

"Slipperiness? Hot slops?"

"A lot of cooking oil and grease goes down, so the ladder is very slippery," explained Crow. "We'll have to climb with a grit bag and grit up every now and then. And sometimes the assistant cooks pour out things like hot soup."

"They might not be cooking with the Icecarl invasion going on," said Tal hopefully.

Crow shook his head at Tal. "They'll be cooking more than ever. Fighters need feeding. But the ladder is on the far side of the shaft from the kitchen hatches, so only a long throw or a lot of stuff coming down could get to us."

Tal thought about it for a moment. There didn't seem to be any alternative. He had to get to the Violet levels as quickly as possible, and from there into the Violet Tower. This slopdown seemed the best and most secret way.

"All right. But you go first."

Crow nodded. "This way," he said. "There's an old kitchen back here somewhere."

Of course, Crow knew exactly where the old kitchen was. Like most places around the Hall of Nightmares, it had not been used in many, many years. The rows of ovens were cold, their Sunstones dead. The cupboards were empty, doors hanging open at odd angles, old hinges giving way.

Crow went to a grey iron hatch in one wall. It was hinged at the bottom, designed to be pulled open and down. Crow tugged at the handle, but it was stuck fast.

Tal and Adras came to help, and they pulled together. There was a grinding noise, then a sudden snap. All three fell over backwards, still holding the handle.

But the hatch was open a fraction. An awful smell came wafting out from behind it. The smell of years-old cooking oil, the odour of ancient, putrefied meat, and the newer but no less disgusting reek of rotten vegetables.

Tal gagged and held his nose. Crow shook his head as if he could shake the smell off. But Adras was affected even worse. He twisted up into a frenzied whirlwind, spinning round and round and roaring incoherently. Whatever he was saying wasn't clear, but his feelings were obvious. Adras was totally repulsed by the slopdown.

"Stop that!" shouted Tal as he ripped one of his sleeves to make a face mask, while Crow did the same with his new black robe. "It's… it's not that bad."

Adras stopped spinning.

"Yes it is," complained the Spiritshadow. "The air is dead and poisoned!"

"It's only food scraps and... and stuff," said Tal bravely. "And it's the quickest way to get to the Violet levels. We have to climb it."

"No," said Adras firmly. "I will go and find Odris."

"You'll get used to the smell," said Crow. "And there will be a bit of fresh air around each kitchen hatch. If they're open."

"Come on, let's get going," said Tal. He knew Adras would follow, no matter what he said. They were bound together. Adras could not go far from him or vice versa. Tal thought his own willpower was stronger. Adras would give in and follow. "You go first, Crow."

Crow nodded. He tied his face mask on and climbed through the hatch. Then he climbed back in.

"Forgot the grit," he said, showing blackened, greasy palms to Tal. "The first few rungs of the ladder are really slippery just here. They usually keep some next to the hatch..."

He rummaged about in the cupboards near the

hatch, and eventually found two mouldy bags of chalklike powder. After testing that the bag was not too rotten, he plunged his hands into it and wrung them, so that he got a good coating of the gritty substance.

"You tie the bag to your belt like this, so that it can still be opened with one hand," he said, showing Tal. "We'll probably have to grit up every level or so."

Tal took the bag, checked it was sound and copied Crow. In the back of his mind he couldn't help thinking that climbing a greasy ladder was the perfect opportunity for Crow to take his revenge. All he had to do was tread on Tal's hands and he'd fall for sure.

"Right, I'll go again," said Crow. "Don't follow too close, in case I slip." He climbed through the hatch and his feet disappeared as he pulled himself up the ladder inside the shaft. His voice came echoing back down, along with another disgusting waft of awful smells.

Tal hesitated. Crow was warning him and he appeared to be more honest and open than he had in the past. But was this all just an act to lull Tal into thinking he was safe?

"I'm not going," said Adras.

"Yes you are," said Tal, his voice very stern. "We don't have a choice. Stop your nonsense and follow me."

He climbed through the hatch. Adras *did* follow him, though the Spiritshadow made a small continuous noise that was very like a small child whining.

The smell was even worse inside, so strong that even with his mask Tal could only take shallow breaths. He knew if he really breathed in hard he would instantly vomit. The shaft was smaller than Tal had expected, and darker. He increased the light from his Sunstone, which was tied into the point of his collar, making it bright enough to shine through the cloth as if it wasn't there.

Crow was already a good twenty stretches higher up and making good progress. Tal watched him climb for a while, noting that the Freefolk boy always made sure he had one really solid hand- and foothold before he took another step.

The rungs were really greasy. If it wasn't for the grit on his hands, Tal wasn't sure he'd be able to hang on.

He looked down for a moment, but quickly looked back up. There was nothing below but darkness, the ladder disappearing out of sight. The smell already made him feel nauseous and looking down didn't help. Besides, with the danger of slops being thrown down from above, he would be much better off looking up.

He looked up and started to climb. It was a long way up to the Violet levels. Even if he didn't fall off on the way, once they got there he'd still have to find a way into the Violet Tower.

Then he would have to confront Sushin and the great shadowdragon who was Sushin's ultimate master.

Sharrakor.

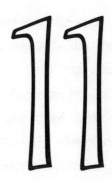

The water was freezing cold. But the Shield Maiden who'd been through once already said that the flooded tunnel was only twelve stretches long before it sloped up into air again.

Twelve stretches wasn't very far, Milla thought. She suppressed a shiver as she took another step and the water rose above her waist. Something rippled in the water next to her and she almost struck at it with the Talon before she realised it was Odris swimming. Even as a Spiritshadow, Odris liked water. It was the stuff of life for a Storm Shepherd in Aenir. Or part of it anyway. Air and water, that's what they were made of. Air, water and magic.

Two Shield Maidens were close behind Milla, helping Graile's Spiritshadow with its mistress, who was still very weak. Milla was pleased with the shimmering globe of green light that surrounded Graile's head. It seemed to be working properly.

She took another step and the water gripped at her neck. It was so cold it constricted her lungs. Still, she told herself, it was not as cold as a windstorm out on the Ice.

Milla breathed in and out slowly, several times. Then she took the breath that would have to last her through the flooded tunnel. As the last of it filled her lungs, she pushed forward, keeping one hand against the wall so she would keep going in the right direction. The water was too dirty and dark to see in, even with a Sunstone.

One step, two steps, three steps... it was hard going, walking underwater. The floor beneath her was slippery too, so she had to be careful. If she slid over, she might get turned around, or smack her head and lose her precious breath.

Four steps... five steps... six steps... that had to

be two stretches, surely? But she'd been taking smaller steps than usual, so maybe it wasn't. Already she felt short of air, the cold pressing on her lungs and throat.

Maybe she'd become weaker since she'd been to Aenir and lost her natural shadow. Maybe wielding the Talon and using Light Magic had weakened her too. She was used to having magical or Spiritshadow help, and some of her toughness had leaked away. Surely such a small crossing underwater wouldn't have worried her before?

Ten steps. Or was it eleven? Milla tried to move faster through the water. Her breath was almost gone and she couldn't bear the shame of drowning – or almost drowning and having to be rescued. That Shield Maiden Jorle had been through twice already and hadn't been bothered at all.

She had to keep going. It could only be a few more steps.

Unless she'd somehow found another branch of the tunnel. What if Jorle had been lucky and gone straight through, but Milla had somehow ended up taking a side passage? Maybe she was walking even deeper underwater, into blacker depths from which there would be no return.

A second later, she burst out into air and light, gasping a heartfelt breath. Ebbitt was standing further up a ramp ahead, the green globe still around his head, not as bright as it had been.

"What took you so long?" he asked. "We have a locomotor to catch."

Milla climbed out of the water and up the ramp to Ebbitt. Then she shook herself, sending a spray across the old man. He flinched and grimaced and muttered about something called *towels*, but didn't retreat.

There was a loud splash below. Graile and the two Shield Maidens emerged – Graile completely calm but shivering, the two Icecarls spluttering and gasping for breath.

As soon as they looked up, Milla slowed her own breathing. She knew that a leader must try to appear calm and capable at all times. But she wasn't sure whether the Shield Maidens were fooled, particularly when they immediately tried to disguise their own panting for more air.

The next Icecarl to arrive was the Wilder, Jarek. He was still emerging from the strange condition that came when the berserk fury left. He seemed unaffected by the crossing, but did not speak or even look at anyone else. He trudged up the ramp and stood cradling his chain, his eyes blank.

Perhaps it was actually grief from the loss of his companion, Milla thought as she cast a cautious glance at him, and not the aftereffects of the fury. She did not know much about Wilders.

"Hurry up, hurry up," chanted Ebbitt. "I told you we have a locomotor to catch."

"This is not a time for hunting. We must get to the Violet levels as quickly as we can," Milla said impatiently. "What is a locomotor anyway? Some sort of beast?"

"You'll see, you'll see," explained Ebbitt. "But it is not for hunting. Oh, no. We will catch it to ride it, and it will take us the first part of the way we have to go to get to where we're going."

"The Violet levels," reiterated Milla. She wanted to be absolutely sure Ebbitt knew where they wanted to go. Though even with constant repetition there was no guarantee.

"We are all here, War-Chief," called Saylsen from the bottom of the ramp. As Milla half expected, the Shield Mother was hardly out of breath and didn't even look as wet, bedraggled and cold as everybody else.

"Come," said Ebbitt. He led the way to the top of the ramp and then along a sandy tunnel that cut straight through the rock, without smooth walls or stonework. There were no Sunstones set in the ceiling here, and the only light came from the stones of Milla and Ebbitt, aided by a dim glow from Graile's.

The tunnel went on for a long way. After a while, Milla heard a strange noise coming from up ahead. It sounded a little like the metalworkers of the Firekeeper Clan, the Icecarls who held the secret of turning rocks into metal. They were the only ones who could use the special rock that was sometimes found around the hot pools of ghalt, or which fell from the sky like Sunstones. The metal they made wasn't as good as the golden metal of the ancients, but it was prized just the same.

The ring of metal and the dull thud of stone grew louder as they kept on. Ebbitt obviously heard it, but was not concerned. Milla decided that if he wasn't, she wouldn't be, either. The Icecarls took their lead from her.

"Careful now," warned Ebbitt. He slowed down and held his Sunstone higher. Milla tensed, her Talon-hand ready. Odris, seeing that, slipped back.

"The tunnel ends above the locomotor road, up ahead," said Ebbitt. "We have to drop into one of the locomotor buckets, which will carry us along to a point where we can go by steam. Some of us, anyway."

"What is a locomotor and what is one of their buckets?" asked Milla.

Ebbitt didn't reply, but he gestured Milla to come and join him. Together, they walked slowly forward. The light from their Sunstones lit the way ahead, the tunnel walls giving way to a much larger open space where their light could only partly banish the darkness.

The tunnel ended at a cliff partway up the side of a large cavern. Below them, on the floor of the cavern, was a strange path that led into the darkness, a path that was marked by three metal lines, each about a stretch apart.

Something moved out of the darkness, something about the size of a juvenile Selski. It took Milla only a moment to recognise that it was not a living thing, but the source of the hammering sound. It was just a box of metal, open at the top, balanced on a platform that had two big wheels running on the outside metal lines. There were also little toothed wheels at each end, clacking along on the metal line in the middle.

"A locomotor bucket," explained Ebbitt. "The locomotor is at the back. It pushes the buckets around on those metal lines, which are called rails. There are many locomotors, each one pushing ten buckets. They come out of the darkness below, rise to where we want to go, and then disappear down into the darkness again."

Milla kept staring as more and more of the wheeled boxes Ebbitt called buckets came into view. As he'd said, there were ten, all of them pushed along by the strange locomotor. Unlike the buckets, the locomotor appeared to be at least partially alive, a thing of strangely pulsing grey flesh that sat on the same kind of wheeled platform. The blob of flesh had powerful arms, each as long as a grown Icecarl, that turned the wheels. But there was no skin covering these limbs. Milla could see the muscles tensing and relaxing, and the sheen of bone.

"Line up along here," Ebbitt instructed. "When an empty bucket is beneath us, we just jump down."

"Where do we get out?" asked Milla. She had a vision of the strange locomotor pushing them somewhere they didn't want to go, deep beneath the Castle.

"There is a place ahead where the line steepens and the locomotors stop to gather their strength," explained Ebbitt. "We jump out there, right next to an Underfolk passage that goes to a steam riser and also out to Red Five."

"Where does the locomotor go after that?"

Ebbitt shrugged. "Down again," he said. "I don't know where. One day I'll find out."

The first bucket drew level with them as Ebbitt finished speaking. It was travelling not much faster than a walk, and was only four or five stretches below. An easy jump for an Icecarl. Even Graile, aided by her Spiritshadow, could do it, Milla thought.

"Everyone line up along the edge here," ordered Milla. "We'll jump in the last two buckets."

"No, not the last two," interrupted Ebbitt. "Stay at least one bucket away from the locomotor."

Milla looked at him.

"It has extra arms as well as the ones that turn the wheels," said Ebbitt. "And somewhere under all that flesh, I believe there is a mouth."

Milla wasn't sure whether to believe him, but it was better to err on the side of safety.

"You have done this before, haven't you?" she asked.

Ebbitt smiled.

"Get ready to jump," said Saylsen, who had kept her eye on the buckets and was timing their passage. "Avoid the last bucket, as instructed."

"You have, haven't you?" Milla asked again.

Ebbitt kept smiling, but made no move to answer.

"Jump!" Saylsen shouted.

12

Tal climbed wearily out of the hatch and fell on to the kitchen floor. It had been a longer climb than he could have imagined, much further than when he had climbed the Red Tower. His hands were raw, blood mixing with the grit, and one shoulder was caked in the foul-smelling residue that had come flying down the shaft when they were about halfway up. Fortunately it had been cold.

Crow was sitting close by, his face pale, obviously even more worn out than Tal. Adras was sliding across the ceiling, trying to get as far away from the odorous slopdown as he could.

Unlike the kitchen they'd left so far below, this

one was still in use. Fires burned under many pots, and there were even some old Sunstone-powered hot plates that glowed yellow and red with permanent heat. A breeze constantly blew through the kitchen, taking smoke and cooking smells up into holes in the ceiling. There were benches laden with fresh ingredients being prepared by Underfolk cooks. Tal saw belish root, cave fish, shrimps, orange and red yaribles, blue mushrooms and more – enough to make him remember he was hungry.

All the Underfolk were gathered at the far end of the kitchen, clearly scared by these garbage-encrusted intruders who had emerged from the slopdown hatch. Tal raised his Sunstone and it flashed Violet. Instantly they all turned back to their allotted tasks, ignoring the unexpected arrivals.

"A flash of light and they know who's master," whispered Crow. But he said it without the anger that would have been there before. He just sounded sad.

Tal looked at the stacked crockery on one of the nearer benches. It was all of violet-coloured crystal, confirming that this was indeed a kitchen on one of the Violet levels.

"Where do we go from here?" asked Crow. "How do we get into the Violet Tower? I hope we don't have to climb the outside of it."

"I'm not sure," Tal admitted. He knew very little about the Violet Tower. He remembered being taught that it was much larger and higher than the other six. But he didn't remember much else. He had seen the topmost part of it briefly from the Red Tower, but it had been the farthest away, and he hadn't been able to make out any details.

"You must have some idea," continued Crow.

"I have one idea," said Tal. "I'm just not sure it's a good one."

Crow looked at him expectantly.

"Well," Tal began, "the Empress must be... must have been able to get into the Violet Tower. And there's a children's puzzle song that might have something to do with it, only I can't remember it properly. It has a line that goes 'The first sat here, the second spied here, the third flew here, the fourth ate here, the fifth was born here, the sixth sang here, and the seventh grew here.' All I can remember of the answering part is that the first was an Emperor, the third a bird – probably a crow, I guess – and then it ends with 'the seventh was a tower'. And 'here' was the Audience Chamber, which has the Imperial Throne in it. Only I don't know where the Audience Chamber is."

"I know who we can ask," said Crow. He slowly got to his feet and looked at the Underfolk, who were keeping their distance. "If the Empress ever ordered a drink or food, someone from here would have taken it to her."

"I guess so," said Tal. He got up too, ignoring the stabbing pains in the muscles of his arms and legs.

Crow singled out the most senior Underfolk, an old cook, and started to talk to him. Tal tried to stretch a bit, to ease the stiffness that he knew would come along sooner or later. He was tired, his weariness made worse by the aftereffects of the water-spider poison. He didn't really listen to Crow and the Underfolk cook until Crow called out to him.

"Tal! Come and hear this."

Tal pushed himself off the bench he was leaning against and walked over. Above his head, Adras glided across the ceiling.

"Tell him what you told me," instructed Crow.

The Underfolk man bowed nervously. He obviously didn't know what to make of Crow and he wasn't absolutely sure about Tal, even with his Sunstone and Spiritshadow.

"As it please you, Masters—"

"Don't call us Masters!" Crow interrupted.

The cook bobbed his head several times and cleared his throat."Yes, Ma— as it pleases you. The Audience Chamber and the Imperial Throne are not used, haven't been used by Her Highness, not these many years. Well, never, I think, as my parents told me."

"But it must be cleaned from time to time," said Crow. "Everywhere is cleaned."

The cook shook his head.

"No, no. The doors cannot be opened, save by the Empress. In my father's time, under the old Emperor, the doors were always open and I am sure we cleaned it most thoroughly. It is not neglect,

Masters, not at all. I am sure the Cleaners would be very happy, most ecstatic to clean the Audience Chamber again…"

"Can you show us where the doors to the Audience Chamber are?" asked Tal. "Can we get to them through Underfolk ways?"

"I am assigned here," said the cook nervously, casting an eye back over all the other Underfolk working over the fires and at the benches. "I cannot leave. But I could send one of our waiters, if it please you, Masters."

"Stop this 'Master' and 'if it pleases you' stuff," said Crow, some of his old anger returning. "You'll be free soon. The Icecarls have invaded the Castle and will win. The Chosen are losing."

The cook trembled at Crow's words and didn't answer. The confusion in his eyes was clear enough. He had only ever known one world and could not imagine it changing.

"A waiter will be fine," said Tal gently. "As long as he knows the way."

The cook bobbed and nodded and hurried off, calling out a name.

"I hope the doors are still closed," said Tal.

"Why?" asked Crow. "How will we get in?"

"I'd forgotten that the Empress never had the Violet Keystone," explained Tal. "Mercur – the old Emperor she deposed – managed to escape with it. He died in the heatways, and that's how we got the stone that Ebbitt split in two for Milla and me."

"So?"

"I bet you need the Violet Keystone to open the doors to the Audience Chamber and to get into the Violet Tower. That's why the doors have been shut since Mercur's time. If they're open now, it means Sushin has already used the half he stole from me to get in."

Crow nodded thoughtfully.

"What do we do if we run into Sushin?" he asked. "I mean, if he's still there?"

"Hit him with everything we can," said Tal. "You can do a Red Ray of Destruction, can't you?"

"Yes," admitted Crow. Even though he was an Underfolk, he had stolen a Sunstone and had been secretly trained by Ebbitt and Lector Jarnil.

"Then do that," said Tal. "There's a spell I've been

meaning to try on him too, if I can do it. The Violet Unravelling."

"What does that do?" asked Crow.

"It dissolves anything it touches," Tal answered grimly. "I only wish I'd been confident enough to try it on him before."

The cook came hurrying back through the kitchen, dodging the workers as they moved between stove and bench and swung open ovens or sharpened knives. A young Underfolk boy, no more than six or seven years old, trailed after him, surreptitiously picking his nose. He stopped when he saw Tal looking at him and whipped his hands behind his back into the approved posture of a servant.

"This is Edol," said the cook. "He will show you through the serving ways to the Audience Chamber."

13

"I can't truly say I have experienced this delightful ride before," replied Ebbitt, a moment after he landed with Milla in the metal bucket. "But I have read about it."

"I hope what you read is true," said Milla. "I do not like travelling this way, stuck to these metal rails. Even a Selski may be steered."

The other Icecarls in the bucket murmured their agreement.

The sloping sides of the bucket were too high to see over easily, so Milla ordered a Shield Maiden to climb up on the broad shoulders of Jarek to look ahead. Odris slid up and poked her head out so she could see, too.

"How will we know when to get out?" asked Milla. "Is there some sign or mark?"

"When the locomotor slows then we will know," said Ebbitt. "If the locomotor speeds, then we have gone past our needs."

Milla scowled and turned away. She had to think. If the main host had indeed arrived below and was attacking, then the rest of her advance guard would be relieved in time. Tal would probably be all right, since Ebbitt was sure Crow would rescue him, and she had a low opinion of Fashnek. But Sushin had half the Violet Keystone and with it he could finally destroy the Veil. He might already have done it, for all they knew down here. Down here in this metal box, trapped travelling in a straight line to who knew where...

"What's ahead?" she suddenly asked.

"It is very dark," answered the Shield Maiden. "I think... I think the rails ahead go down."

"Down?" asked Ebbitt and Milla at the same time.

"Yes," answered the Shield Maiden. "Definitely. I

can see a locomotor ahead, but not the buckets it pushes – now it has disappeared too. It must be a steep slope."

"Perhaps I misremembered," mused Ebbitt, ducking his head and scratching under his breastplate. "Was it *ascends* or *descends* for the Underfolk corridor I mentioned before? Ascends, descends, upends, depends… oops—"

He turned to Milla and bowed deeply.

"I fear, my dear, that I have been unclear. We need to disembark from this equipage before it *descends*."

"Our first bucket is already over the edge," reported the Shield Maiden.

"Everybody out!" Milla shouted. "Jump!"

She jumped up and got astride the rim of the bucket, swinging her legs over to jump clear. Icecarls jumped around her, but at the last instant Milla hesitated. Someone was missing. She looked back down and saw Graile still lying there, asleep, with her Spiritshadow sprawled next to her.

Milla looked ahead. The next bucket had started down the slope. It had to be an almost vertical drop, she realised, as the buckets disappeared immediately from sight.

"Graile!"

The Chosen did not stir.

Milla jumped back inside, shouting for Odris.

"What?" came a plaintive cry from the Spiritshadow, calling from some distance back along the path. She had obeyed Milla's order to jump.

"Come here!" screamed Milla. "Now!"

She bent down and shook Graile hard, but still the Chosen didn't stir. She was breathing, but deeply unconscious.

Milla heard another bucket go over the edge, the regular clacking of the third wheel replaced by a much higher pitched and more frequent screeching.

She slapped Graile then, but the Chosen woman would not wake. Her Spiritshadow did not move.

"Odris!"

"I'm here," grumbled Odris, who was hovering overhead. "No need to shout."

Milla dragged Graile on to her shoulder. She was surprisingly light for her size, but even so, she was too heavy to boost up over the rim of the bucket.

"Take her," ordered Milla.

Odris dropped down and grabbed Graile with her two puffy arms. As she started to rise again, she gave out a surprised yelp.

"She's stuck," announced Odris. At the same time, Milla heard another bucket go over the edge. That was the third, and they were in the sixth. There were only five or six breaths before they would go over, too.

"What do you mean?" Milla asked frantically. Then she saw what Odris meant. Graile's Spiritshadow was holding on to her with one claw, somehow weighing them both down. "Try harder!"

"I can't move!" wailed Odris. "The Spiritshadow has done something weird – it's too heavy!"

"Leave her!" shouted another voice. Saylsen. The Shield Mother had jumped back on to the side of the bucket and was looking down. "Leave her, War-Chief!"

Another bucket went over. Number four. Milla stood motionless, her mind travelling as fast as it had ever done.

"Light, Odris! What light is best for Spiritshadows? To make you strong?"

"I don't know!" shrieked Odris. "Can I let go?"

"Think! What colour light?"

"White!"

"Look away, Saylsen!"

Milla pointed her Sunstone at Graile's great bird Spiritshadow and thought of pure, white light, the brightest she could imagine. At the same time she turned her head away and lidded her eyes.

Light burst out of the Sunstone. Pure bright light that lit up the bucket and the cavern beyond and made the two Spiritshadows stand out as if they were cut from black cloth and stuck on a whitewashed wall.

Graile's Spiritshadow stirred and flexed its wings. One eye opened and it moved its beak.

"Jump, War-Chief!" pleaded Saylsen. Her cry was immediately followed by the sound of the fifth bucket going over the edge.

They were next.

Still Milla kept the light pouring into Graile's

Spiritshadow. She raised her other arm and called to Odris.

"Odris! Lift me out!"

Odris swooped, Saylsen jumped, and the bucket started to tip. Graile slid down to the end, as Milla leaped into the air and Odris lifted her up. The white light snapped off, and the topmost rim of the bucket clipped Milla's boots as Odris groaned and carried her free.

They landed in a heap only a few stretches from the edge of the cliff, as the seventh bucket went over.

Saylsen was there, already back on her feet. But there was no sign of Graile or her Spiritshadow.

Milla hobbled to the edge of the cliff and looked down. It was a vertical drop, and it went down as far as she could see in the light from her Sunstone. Somehow the locomotor and its buckets stuck to the metal rails. But whatever was in the buckets would almost certainly fall out, down to a distant death.

Milla was suddenly furious with Ebbitt. She had put up with his meandering, crazy ways, but now his absentmindedness had got his own brother's daughter killed. She turned back from the cliff edge to find him... just in time to see an extra arm come out from the locomotor that was approaching. A pink and grisly arm fifteen stretches long that ended in a three-fingered hand the size of a human torso, a hand that was about to grab Saylsen as the locomotor trundled past.

"Ware foe!" shouted Milla and she ran forward, the Talon extending from her outstretched hand.

Saylsen whirled, knives ready, even as the hand closed around her. She stabbed at it over and over again, sending out spouts of grey, watery blood. But the locomotor did not let go and the last bucket went over the cliff and the locomotor began to tip up as Milla reached it and struck.

A brilliant line of light shot out of the Talon and whipped across the creature's wrist. Sparks shot out everywhere, momentarily blinding Milla. She threw herself to the ground in case another arm attacked her while she couldn't see, and rolled further away from the cliff edge.

When her vision cleared, she saw Saylsen

struggling on the ground, the severed locomotor hand still gripping her tight. Milla got up and rushed towards her, in case the hand was somehow strangling the Shield Mother even after it was cut off.

Then she heard movement behind her, the sudden rush of displaced air. Thinking the locomotor had somehow reversed, Milla flung herself aside and spun around, the Talon ready.

But it was not the locomotor.

It was Graile's Spiritshadow, its huge wings fully extended for the first time Milla had seen. It rose above the metal lines, wings beating furiously, then glided in to hover well clear of Milla and her Talon. The Spiritshadow held Graile tenderly in its claws. It hovered in place for a few seconds, then gently deposited the Chosen on the ground and slid down next to her.

Only then did Graile wake up. She stretched and yawned, then looked around with puzzled eyes. She saw Milla, and Saylsen clambering out of the locomotor's severed hand, and Ebbitt and the rest of the Icecarls hurrying up from where they'd jumped.

"I'm sorry," she said. "I fell asleep. Did I miss something?"

Edol led Tal and Crow through a series of ever-narrowing corridors used by the Underfolk waiters. It became clear why the waiters were mainly young children, as there were several places where Tal and Crow had to crawl or squeeze through gaps as the serving way ran under floors or inside a wall. Sometimes there were peepholes to look through, or hatches where food could be left, but Edol led them at a cracking pace and there was no time to steal a glance.

Finally they came to an intersection of four equally narrow corridors. Edol pointed along the left-hand one, which ended in a small door, and said, "Through there's the Grand Parade. Doors to the Audience Chamber across the Grand Parade."

Then he scampered away along the opposite corridor, his forefinger already jammed in his nose again.

Crow squeezed along the corridor, Tal following a little way behind, with Adras at his shoulder. Tal still wanted to keep Crow in front, where he could see him, though the Freefolk leader had behaved perfectly so far.

"Dark take that boy!" swore Crow softly as he examined the door.

"What is it?"

"This isn't really a door," said Crow. "It's a hole in the wall, with a painting or something hung over it. I'm going to have to push the painting off the wall and it's bound to make a noise. If there's anyone on the Grand Parade they'll know about it."

"You can't lift it off quietly?" asked Tal.

"No. It's too heavy."

"Can you cut through it?" asked Tal, thinking of the portraits of former Lectors that were hung in the Lectorium. They were painted on cloth stretched on metal frames.

Crow tapped the obstruction again and shook his head.

"It's made of something solid. I think... I think it's a thin sheet of metal. It might even be a mirror."

"I guess we'll just have to risk it," Tal said finally. "And hope that everyone is down fighting Icecarls."

Crow nodded and began to push at the top of the sheet. It slowly shifted, with a screeching sound that set Tal's hair on edge.

"Hurry up!" he said. The continuous screech of metal on stone was bad enough, let alone any other noise. "Adras, help him!"

Adras flowed around Tal and pushed with his huge puffy arms. Almost immediately the screeching stopped and the whole sheet of metal fell forward, letting in bright Violet-tinged Sunstone light from the broad corridor beyond.

Crow, Tal and Adras watched the rectangle of metal fall, all of them tensed for the sound it would make. But none of them was prepared for the tremendous crash that did eventuate, nor the ringing sound that continued afterward, a ringing that echoed everywhere.

Light flashed everywhere too, for the sheet *was* a mirror of highly polished silver. It quivered on the floor, sending wild flashes in all directions.

"Quick!" said Tal, and the three of them squeezed out into the Grand Parade. With the ringing still in their ears, they looked every which way for possible enemies and somewhere to run to.

Then they all stopped and stared.

Diagonally opposite them were two enormous arched doors. They were made of the ancients' golden metal, but studded with tiny Sunstones so that they shone in all colours, ripples of rainbow light constantly shimmering across their surface.

Both doors were partly open. But neither the Sunstone-laden doors nor the fact that they were open had stopped Tal and Crow in their tracks.

It was the piled-up bodies of dead Chosen sprawled in front of the doors. More than a dozen of them, including Chosen in Violet robes and guards. There was no sign of any Spiritshadows.

The last echo faded away and the silver mirror lay still.

"Sushin did get here first," said Crow.

Tal nodded and tore his gaze away, to check along the Grand Parade. He'd never been here before, though he had come to the Violet levels once. The Grand Parade lived up to its name, as a sweeping, broad corridor that went for stretches and stretches in either direction, before it curved away.

There was no one in sight, at least no one alive. Tal went forward to examine the dead Chosen. They all looked surprised, rather than afraid. None of them had Sunstones in their hands, or anywhere visible, and the guards' swords were still sheathed. There was also no obvious cause of death. No wounds, no burn marks, no other signs of fatal Light Magic.

"I wonder why he killed them," muttered Tal as he moved between the bodies, Crow close by his side, both of them with their Sunstones held ready. "And how."

A slight movement near one of the doors made

them spin nervously, red light flashing in their Sunstones. One of the guards, propped up against the wall, was not dead after all and she had moved her hand.

Tal recognised her. It was Ethar, a Shadowlord of the Violet and a senior officer of the guard. Her hand twitched again and Tal realised she was trying to get him to approach.

"Who walks there?" whispered the woman, raising her head a little. Her eyes did not focus on anything. With a start of horror, Tal knew she was blind.

"Tal Graile-Rerem," he said, stepping over a body to get closer. He was still ready for a sudden attack, but he did not think one would come. At least not from Ethar. Her face was as pallid as the dead Chosen and he knew she would not live long.

A momentary smile crossed Ethar's lips.

"The Beastmaker boy," she said, and coughed. With the cough came a froth of bright red blood that bubbled out of the corner of her mouth. "You played well."

"Did Sushin do this?" asked Tal. "Has he gone

into the Audience Chamber?"

Ethar did not answer immediately. Her chest heaved and more blood stained her lips. Then she said, "Yes and yes. We protested, for all that he was the Dark Vizier and could command us, he had no right to try the doors... He showed us the Violet Keystone and told us to be silent, that he would be Emperor and do as he willed. But even with the Keystone, the Assembly must decide, and we told him... we told him he could not pass."

Tal waited as she stopped and drew in a racking breath.

"He blinded us then, with the Keystone, and in the darkness spoke words, words that felled our Spiritshadows in an instant. I felt my Kerukar go, torn away from me, and I almost went with him. But I did not. Duty... it is my duty... You must stop him, Tal, for he should not be Emperor... He must not be..."

"I will stop him, if I can," said Tal.

"I ask one small boon before you go," whispered Ethar. "From one player to another. End this game."

"What… what do you mean?" asked Tal, but he knew what she meant.

"A Red Ray," whispered Ethar, her hand crawling across to tap weakly against her heart. "Here. Do not let me linger."

Tal raised his Sunstone. Red light swirled inside it, building in intensity. Then a single thin ray snapped out, striking Ethar exactly where she'd indicated. Her body jerked, then slowly subsided down the wall.

Tal wiped his eyes and turned away.

"I never did… I never did kill anyone, you know," said Crow quietly. "Not a single Chosen, for all my talk. I couldn't do what you… I couldn't…"

"I couldn't either," croaked Tal. "Before I met the Icecarls, before… before everything."

Crow was about to say something else when Adras suddenly reared up and looked down the Grand Parade.

"What is it?" asked Tal. "Is someone coming?"

"Yes," said Adras. "A monster."

15

Milla looked at the steps going down, the steps going up, and the narrow passageway that led further on, while Ebbitt hesitated at the intersection, scratching his head.

"Where do we go from here?" asked Milla. "Think carefully, Ebbitt. I don't want down when it should be up, or left when it should be right. You almost got Graile killed!"

"A failing of mine," sighed Ebbitt. "Perhaps if I tied ribbons of different colours to my wrists, I might know left from right. But I am *absolutely* sure of our whereabouts now and about where we shall go. Though I'm afraid only four of us can travel by steam to the Violet levels. Everyone else will have to take those stairs back down to Red Five. I am sure it will be in Icecarl hands by now."

"Why only four?" asked Milla. "And what do you mean to 'travel by steam'?"

"Only four will fit in the envelope," said Ebbitt. "Which is propelled upward by steam rising in the aptly named risers. Though the return pipes for the condensed water are not called fallers, which is strange—"

"Fit in the envelope? What is an envelope? Something like those metal buckets?"

"Not at all," replied Ebbitt. "An envelope is what you put a letter in. An appropriate envelope, depending on the letter. A formal response to an invitation, for example, should be placed inside a square envelope that is either the colour of your order, or white, if seeking to depress pretension—"

"Ebbitt!" snapped Milla. "What is this envelope we can travel in?"

"Oh, that is an envelope of Light Magic. Otherwise we would get scalded by the steam. It is an invention of my own. I suppose it could be called a caul, or a second skin, or a container, or a shroud, though that is rather morbid…"

Ebbitt's voice trailed off into a mutter and he started counting on his fingers, enumerating all the things you could call this envelope of magic he used to travel by steam.

"Perhaps we should try to find some other way," said Milla to Saylsen and Malen. "Graile? Do you know what Ebbitt means? And if we can get out to Red Five we could get to the Violet levels from there, surely?"

Graile was half asleep again, but she opened her eyes as Milla spoke and answered softly, "I don't know exactly what Ebbitt means, but I presume he has found some way to travel through the heating system of the Castle. There are steam pipes that carry steam from the depths throughout the Castle. But yes, if you can get out to the Red levels, there are many ways from there to the Violet levels."

"But not as quickly as by steam," interrupted Ebbitt. "You would have to fight every stretch of the way through Orange, Yellow, Green, Blue, Indigo. By steam, we would be in Violet in a matter of minutes.

Oh, dark take it, I've lost my count. Where was I? Yes, forty-three, a sac, forty-four, a paldroon…"

"I suppose we will have to chance this steam passage," sighed Milla. "I will go, of course, and Malen, you had best come with me. That leaves one to choose. Perhaps Graile…"

But Graile was asleep again, slumped against her Spiritshadow, which had folded one dark wing over her as if she were a chick to be sheltered.

"No. She is still too weak," Milla answered herself.

"I will come, War-Chief," said Saylsen. Milla shook her head. Even though Saylsen had said nothing, Milla was sure from her slightly odd posture that the locomotor hand had broken some of the Shield Mother's ribs, if not inflicted more serious injuries.

"No. I need you to lead the others back to the main host and assume command. I think… Jarek."

"War-Chief—" Saylsen began, but Milla cut her off with a sign.

"We will face the strongest Light Magic," she said. "Jarek can survive it, as we have seen."

"He is a Wilder, War-Chief," warned Saylsen, ignoring Milla's attempt to cut her off. "If the fury takes him, you might not be able to steer him straight. It were best I come with you instead."

Milla met the Shield Mother's fierce gaze and tried to look commanding. But was Saylsen right? Someone had to lead the others back and Milla was sure Saylsen needed to have her ribs bandaged, or perhaps even to be taken back out to the Crones waiting in the heatways.

"I have spoken," she said finally. "You will lead the others back. I will take Malen and Jarek with me."

For a moment, Milla thought Saylsen would refuse, and she wondered what she could do about it. Then the Shield Mother dropped her gaze and clapped her fists.

"As the War-Chief wills," she said. "We will hurry, and I will join the host. We will meet again in the Violet levels, as soon as may be."

"Malen?" asked Milla, to be sure the Crone – and all the other Crones – would not object to this plan.

Malen's eyes clouded for a moment, making

contact. Then she shook her head, rather dispiritedly. She had not been the same since she had been cut off from the group consciousness of the Crones earlier. Some vital spark of life appeared to have gone out of her.

"You are War-Chief," Malen said shortly and clapped her fists. "You will be unfettered by my counsel."

"Jarek?" asked Milla, raising her voice. "I want you to come with me."

Jarek strode through the Shield Maidens, standing out head and shoulders above them all, his strange blue skin glistening in the light from Milla's Sunstone.

The Wilder had finally come out of his post-fury state. He stopped in front of Milla, towering above her, and clapped his fists together. He did not speak, but simply nodded very slowly to indicate that he had heard and would obey.

"Good hunting," said Saylsen and she clapped her fists again, before leading the remaining Shield Maidens and hunters down the steps. Each of them clapped his or her fists as they passed Milla, and she answered in kind. The last two helped Graile up, her Spiritshadow flitting backward and forward behind her.

Graile weakly gave light from her Sunstone to Milla.

"May the Light protect you," she said. "If… if you should meet up with Tal, tell him that he has my love, trust and hope. May we all meet again, under the Veil."

"That is also my wish," said Milla. "We will do everything we can to secure the Veil."

"Farewell, Uncle," Graile added as she started down the stairs. But Ebbitt didn't hear her. He was in a world of his own, mumbling and counting, until Milla tapped him on the shoulder.

"We are ready," she said. "Take us to the steam and the Violet levels."

16

For once Ebbitt was right about where they were. He led Milla and the others further along the passage that ended in a small room totally dominated by a large metal door, with a wheel set in the middle of it.

"Here we are, here we are," declared Ebbitt. "Gather close, everyone, gather close. No, closer still, please, Master Blue. Odris, you do not need to join us. Steam does not hurt shadows."

Jarek did not seem displeased by being called Master Blue, Milla was relieved to see. They all clustered close around Ebbitt. When they'd finished shuffling and were all practically shoulder to shoulder, the old Chosen raised his hand and the Sunstone ring on his finger suddenly shone with a pure indigo light.

"One, two, around Master Blue," chanted Ebbitt, moving his hand in a complex gesture, a trail of light following the motion. "Three, four, can't take any more."

Milla watched with interest as Ebbitt used the light like a weaver would a shuttle, building up threads of light into a solid cloth that wrapped all around the four of them. It extended under their feet too, and finished with Ebbitt bringing it in over the top as well.

"Walk with me, stay near," ordered Ebbitt. He shuffled towards the metal door. Then he pushed his hands against the indigo light that surrounded them and it stretched out without breaking, giving Ebbitt indigo mittens. He turned the wheel, but did not open the door, looking to his Spiritshadow.

It looked back, then slowly slipped under the door. This was not made of the golden metal, Milla observed, for that was impervious to shadows, and there was no crack between floor and door. It was merely iron or something similar.

The feline Spiritshadow did not return for a minute or two. Ebbitt tapped his foot impatiently and whistled through his teeth. Finally the Spiritshadow slipped back out and nodded its great maned head.

Ebbitt opened the door and steam poured out all over them. The three Icecarls started, but the steam was repelled by the indigo light, splashing harmlessly around them.

Beyond the door, Milla could just see a deep shaft, filled with steam. Obviously this was one of the risers Ebbitt had mentioned.

"In step now," said Ebbitt. "Don't think we'll fall, because we have a very pretty floor."

He stepped off with the others shuffling behind. For an instant he looked like he would fall, despite his words, with the indigo light giving way under his feet. But it simply bounced a little and supported both him and the others as they followed him into the shaft. The two Spiritshadows slid along the wall and then slowly slipped through the envelope of light that surrounded Ebbitt and the Icecarls.

"It tickles," giggled Odris as she rose up next to Milla. "Tickly light."

"Great gouts of steam," muttered Ebbitt as he shuffled around and closed the door behind them, the indigo light still wrapping his hands when he pushed against it. "Huge great gusts of great steam. That's what we want."

Nothing happened for another minute.

"Gigantic gusts," said Ebbitt hopefully. "Super surges. Gales. Hurricanoes."

Still nothing happened.

"What is wrong with the stupid steam system!" Ebbitt shouted. He knelt down and put his ear to the glowing floor of light. "Come, steam! Come!"

Milla opened her mouth to ask Ebbitt what he was doing, but before she could speak, a titanic force hit the envelope and threw them all against the walls and floor as they accelerated at a speed none of the Icecarls could have imagined. Desperately, they clung to one another and tried to get upright again as the envelope rocketed up.

"Steam, glorious steam, there's nothing quite

white as it," sang Ebbitt. Then he started counting very loudly.

It was hard to hear him, with the roar of the steam and the whoosh the envelope made as they went faster and faster and faster. Milla began to worry that they would collide with something at the very top of the shaft and be splintered into pieces, like an iceship running into a rock under full sail.

As Ebbitt counted, "Sixty!" he grabbed the indigo wall in front of him and pulled it in as hard as he could, to let the steam that had propelled them rush past the envelope. At the same time, his Spiritshadow sank its rear claws into the floor and reached out through the light to sink its front claws into the stone wall of the shaft. With a terrible bone-tingling screech the envelope skidded to a halt, with everyone ending up tumbled together on the floor.

"Perfect!" declared Ebbitt proudly as he crawled out from under Milla and Malen. He reached across, the light stretching around his hands, and grasped the locking wheel of another door. "Violet One, as promised."

"Stand ready!" ordered Milla sharply as Ebbitt

spun the wheel. She raised her hand and the Talon started to glow with its harsh red-gold light. Jarek unwound his chain. Malen stepped behind them.

Steam spiralled out as they left the riser and stepped out into an antechamber with a corridor beyond. Ebbitt slammed the door behind them, spun the wheel, then waited a few seconds for the steam to dissipate before dismissing the protective envelope with a pulse of multicoloured light from his Sunstone.

There was no sign of any Chosen or Underfolk. Jarek went to the corner and looked out cautiously, then signed that there were no enemies in sight.

"Right here," said Ebbitt. He pointed left with his right hand, then he used his left hand to pick up his right hand and point it right. "That way."

"Lead on, Jarek," ordered Milla.

"This will take us to the Grand Parade," said Ebbitt. "From there we can get to the Audience Chamber and Milla can open the doors for us."

Milla nodded. She didn't ask Ebbitt why she would have to open the doors. It was better not to ask. He would probably want her to sweep the floor next.

17

"A *blue* monster," added Adras.

Tal and Crow huddled down behind the bodies and Adras slid to the wall as they watched a huge, manlike creature come cautiously around the bend in the Grand Parade. He was bright blue and had shimmering, metallic legs. He carried what looked like a chain in his hand.

"What is it?" asked Tal.

Crow stood up. He seemed nervous, but in a strange way.

"Jarek!" he called. "We're friends."

"What are you doing?" hissed Tal. He felt a momentary panic. This was where Crow betrayed him. He had to do something before—

Someone else came around the bend, following the blue man. Tal started in recognition, forgetting all thoughts of Crow and his possible treachery. He'd know that white-blonde hair anywhere, even if it was topped by something that looked like a crown. That was part of being War-Chief of the Icecarls, he supposed.

He was about to stand up and shout, "Milla!" when a shadow flashed past him, bellowing like thunder, his arms spread wide.

"Odris!"

This shout was met with the cry of "Adras!" and an answering shadow leaped into the air from behind Milla. The two of them met halfway, with a clap of thunder that shook the mirror on the floor again and made both Tal and Milla wince as they shared the shock of the Storm Shepherds' meeting.

Shouting "Milla!" after that seemed a bit pointless. Instead Tal got up slowly and walked forward. He felt strangely nervous. He hadn't seen Milla since they'd parted company down in the Underfolk levels, he to climb the Red Tower again and she to go to the Ice. An awful lot had happened since then. To both of them, it seemed.

To make matters worse, Tal realised he had never really been sure whether they were friends or not. They had been comrades in adversity, but had also fought and troubled each other a lot. What was going to happen now? Maybe Milla still wanted to kill him, as she had when they'd first met...

Milla was thinking similar thoughts as she watched Tal approach. She wasn't certain of her own feelings. There was a familiar irritation at the sight of him, but that was coupled with a relief that he was still alive and looked unscathed from the Hall of Nightmares.

They met in the middle of the corridor, ignoring their two Spiritshadows, who were still spinning around and chasing each other up and down the corridor in sheer joy.

"Milla," said Tal, and stopped.

"Tal," replied Milla.

A heavy silence fell between them, then both spoke at once.

"I'm glad you're alive," said Tal.

"I met your mother," said Milla.

"My mother! Is she all right? I wasn't sure if the antidote—"

"She is weak, but well, and under our protection down in the conquered levels. She sends you her love and knows you will do what must be done."

"Sushin has the Violet Keystone – my half, I mean," said Tal hurriedly. It seemed easier to talk about that than anything personal. "He will use it to destroy the Veil. We have to stop him."

"We know," said Milla, with that calm, confident tone that always annoyed him. "That's why we're here. Where is Sushin?"

"Um, I don't know," replied Tal awkwardly. "We only just got here. But he's opened up the Audience Chamber and probably got into the Violet Tower already, so we have to hurry."

"Then why are we standing and talking?" snapped Milla. She turned back and shouted, "Hurry up!"

She pushed past Tal and strode down towards the open doors.

The enormous blue man who had stood behind her looked at Tal, a look that scared and shook him. There was madness deep in his eyes, and Tal knew it could erupt into full force at any time.

"You must be Jarek," he said weakly and clapped his fists together. "I'm Tal. I'm a... sort of honorary Far-Raider..."

Jarek did not return the greeting, but continued after Milla.

Tal was just about to follow him in turn when he saw Ebbitt and another Icecarl, a young woman who must have been some sort of apprentice Crone or something. She had Crone robes on anyway, though her eyes were a remarkably bright blue.

"Great-uncle Ebbitt!" Tal called and ran over to him, embracing the old man with sudden fervour. "I am so glad I didn't kill you!"

"Then let go," replied Ebbitt. "Before you strangle me to make sure of your botched job."

Tal laughed and let go. He suddenly felt so much better. Having Milla and Ebbitt with him made the odds so much better for facing Sushin.

"This is the Crone Malen," said Ebbitt. "Very

interesting person. Could teach you a thing or two."

"Uh, I'm s-sure," stammered Tal. He clapped his fists to her too, and unlike Jarek, she answered, though it was more automatic than heartfelt.

"I know much about you," said Malen coolly.

"From Milla?" asked Tal.

"No," said Malen. "The War-Chief has not the time for speaking tales. I have walked through her mind, with the other Crones. I have seen her memories, seen Aenir through her eyes, and you."

"Oh, good," said Tal weakly as he tried to remember how he would have showed up in Milla's memories. Not too well, he suspected.

"Ebbitt, Sushin has the Violet Sunstone," he said as they hurried after Milla. "And the Empress and the Light Vizier are dead, and they told me that Sushin is the shadow-pawn of Sharrakor—"

"Shadow-pawn? Shadow-pawn?" exploded Ebbitt. "They said that?"

"Yes," replied Tal, surprised by the violence of the old man's reaction. "What does it mean?"

"No idea," said Ebbitt. "But it sounds bad."

"Hello, Tal."

"Oh, hello, Odris," replied Tal, waving at the Spiritshadow above him.

"Adras says you went back to Aenir and you stuck him in a funny suit and he got eaten by a thing and then when you returned here he got put in a box and after that he had to climb up a really smelly pipe," said Odris sternly. "You should be more careful with him. He has a weak constitution."

"I will be more careful," said Tal mechanically. Somehow this reunion wasn't going as well as might be expected. "Ebbitt, do you know how to get into the Violet Tower?"

"I have an inkling or two," said Ebbitt. He looked down and tugged his crystal breastplate away from his chest, a strange gesture that Tal supposed was meant to be an indication of modesty – or maybe was just a new kind of twitch.

"Lokar is free, by the way," continued Tal earnestly. "She's going to try and replace the Red Keystone. She said that it might be able to keep the Veil going for a little while even if the Violet Keystone is unsealed."

"Lokar is the Guardian of the Red Keystone?" asked Ebbitt, raising one frosty eyebrow. "Lokar! Whoever will they think of next?"

"But you knew that," said Tal. "She's Lector Jarnil's cousin..."

His voice trailed off as they reached the doors and he stepped inside for the first time.

Into the Audience Chamber. Into a vast hall, as large or larger than the Assembly of the Chosen he knew down in the colourless midsection of the Castle between Yellow and Green.

The Audience Chamber had a domed ceiling that was bright with thousands of Sunstones around the rim, but stretched into darkness at its apex. The floor was tiled in all seven colours of the spectrum, but every eighth tile was a mirror, reflecting the light from the Sunstones that rimmed the dome, so that light flowed and shimmered everywhere, making it very difficult to see anything in the huge room.

Tal shielded his eyes with his arm. He could make out Milla, Jarek and Crow ahead of him, and there was some sort of construction right in the middle of the chamber, but that was all. He could not see Sushin, or any other doors, stairs or other exits or entrances. There was no clear way from here to the Seventh Tower.

"Come," said Ebbitt, seeing the question on his face. "The answer lies in the throne."

The lonely structure in the centre of the Audience Chamber was the Imperial Throne of the Chosen. Carved from a single rainbow crystal, it was an ornate and enormous chair wide enough to seat three people. The back of it rose ten stretches from the seat and was finger-thin. Light shone through it as if it were a thick pane of beautiful, multicoloured glass.

A ring of Sunstones was set in the floor around the throne – large, violet Sunstones soldered in place with gold.

"So what is the answer?" asked Tal as they all stood looking at the throne. He also cast a suspicious eye at the ring of Sunstones. They were too big and too purposefully placed to be decorative. They had some function, probably defensive. They might project heat or flame, or something equally dangerous.

"The way to the Violet Tower," said Ebbitt, "lies on the throne. Though only the bearer of the Violet Keystone may use it."

Tal looked at Milla. He felt ashamed – Milla would never have lost her half of the Keystone to Sushin and she probably despised him for letting their enemy get such a vital thing.

Milla met his gaze. Then she twisted the Sunstone ring off her finger and threw it to him.

He caught it reflexively, more surprised than he ever had been in his life.

"Milla!" exclaimed Malen. "What are you doing?"

"Returning the Emperor of the Chosen's Keystone," said Milla calmly. "Though I would like your other Sunstone in return, Tal."

Wordlessly, Tal threw her the Sunstone he had taken from Fashnek. Then he slipped on the half Keystone. It pulsed with sudden Violet, a light that was answered by the ring of stones in the floor.

"Take it back," said Malen, her voice cool. Her eyes were cloudy, Tal saw. She was communing with the other Crones. "The stone is the Icecarls' now. Take it back, War-Chief."

Jarek grunted and started towards Tal, but stopped as Milla raised her hand.

"I do not know how to use it to its fullest strength," she said, speaking not to the Crone in front of her but all the other Crones beyond. "Tal has the power and the right. What is more important? Squabbles between Icecarls and Chosen, or saving the Veil?"

Malen was silent. Tal could not know what was happening, but Milla did. The Crones were arguing among themselves and needed to vote.

"How exactly does the throne tie in with the way to the Seventh Tower?" whispered Tal to Ebbitt as the silence dragged on.

Ebbitt shrugged. Tal noticed the old man was keeping a wary eye on Jarek.

"Sit on it and we'll both find out," whispered Ebbitt.

Malen coughed. Everybody stood absolutely still. Jarek's chain slowly unfolded from his hand, link by clanking link.

"Very well, War-Chief," Malen said in the strange combination voice of the massed Crones, her words echoing through the chamber. "Once more we follow your lead. We have chosen well."

Trust the Crones to congratulate themselves for giving in, thought Milla.

"Thank you," Tal said to Milla. "Ebbitt thinks I should sit on the throne."

"We should all sit on it," said Ebbitt, who was peering down at the Sunstones in the floor, then back up at the dome high above them. "Tal, you go first."

Tal looked at the Sunstones in the floor too, and remembered his earlier thoughts. To be on the safe side, he summoned Violet from the Keystone once more, letting it wash all over him. Then he stepped across the ring.

The stones in the floor glowed, but did nothing else, not even when Ebbitt and the others followed Tal.

The throne was cold and hard. There was a dusty cushion on the seat, but it had long lost any comfort it once offered and was so dusty that Tal sneezed every time he moved even slightly.

Ebbitt came and sat on his left, and Milla on his right. Crow crouched next to Ebbitt, and Malen squeezed in beside Milla. Jarek knelt down in front of Milla and Malen, watching Tal balefully. Ebbitt's maned cat flung itself down in front of the throne, under all their feet. Adras and Odris drifted up to hang on either side of the throne's back, like strange heraldic retainers.

"Bit crowded," remarked Tal. "What do I do now?"

No one answered.

"Great-uncle Ebbitt? What do I do now?"

"You're the Emperor," snapped Ebbitt. "How would I know? Do something imperial, you idiot."

Tal bit back a hasty reply. If he was the Emperor, surely he deserved to be addressed as something more respectful than "you idiot". Not that there was much hope of that from Ebbitt.

Still, perhaps the advice was good, however it was offered. Tal raised his hand and summoned forth more Violet, sending a beam of it straight at the circle of Sunstones on the floor.

The stones answered immediately, flaring so brightly that everyone had to shield their eyes. At the same time, the Sunstones in the rim of the dome shone brighter and rays of Violet struck down. Hundreds of distinct rays, from every part of the rim, connected with the circle around the throne.

"Well done," said Ebbitt.

"It looks pretty," said Tal dubiously, watching the dust rise through the Violet streams. "But it doesn't seem to be doing anything."

"Apart from lifting us up, you mean?" asked Milla.

Tal looked at her, then back down at the floor. As usual she was right. The throne and the circle of floor around it were slowly rising towards the dome, suspended on the hundreds of beams of Violet from the rim. They were already a good twenty stretches up.

"Yes," he said weakly. "Apart from that."

"Well, the dome is opening at the top," added

Crow. "I suppose that could be counted as something else. I guess that's how we get to the bottom of the Violet Tower."

"Sure to be," said Tal, trying to sound confident. "But Sushin may have set some sort of trap there, or he might be there himself still. We'll have to be careful."

Silently and steadily, the throne continued to rise. Tal tried not to think of what might happen if the magic failed part of the way up. Odris and Adras might be fast enough to save him and Milla, but the others would fall to their deaths. They were already a hundred... no, a hundred and fifty stretches up... with a hundred to go and a very hard floor below.

The magic did not fail. The throne passed through the circular gap in the dome and came to rest in another, much smaller room. It was also completely bare and there were far fewer Sunstones set in the ceiling. A broad staircase made from a pale green, highly polished stone wound up in one corner.

"Welcome to the Seventh Tower," said Tal as they

stepped off the throne and walked towards the stairs.

His voice sounded strange and doom-laden, even to him, and he wished he hadn't spoken.

19

As soon as Tal left the circle of Sunstones, the throne began to sink again, back down to the Audience Chamber. Ebbitt, who had been lingering, had to jump out, assisted by his Spiritshadow, who lifted him by his collar much as it would carry a kitten.

There was no sign of Sushin or any visible trap. Even so, Milla gestured to Jarek to go ahead of them, up the green stone stairs. He was not only tough enough to withstand a light trap, but was also a very experienced hunter, likely to detect any ambush.

The stair led up to another level, and another

chamber that was empty and bare. But the stair did not continue further and there were four large doors to choose for further exploration. All the doors were made of the golden metal, Tal noticed, and the walls were also lined with a close mesh of golden metal against the stone. No Spiritshadows could pass through doors or walls here.

"Dark take it!" swore Tal. They couldn't afford any delay by going the wrong way. "That's all we need. Which one do we take?"

"Just follow Sushin," said Ebbitt. "Elementary tracking, my boy."

Tal looked at the stone beneath his feet and stamped in exasperation. As he'd expected, even stamping left no mark on this floor. There wouldn't be any tracks to follow.

Or so he thought, until he saw Jarek at one of the doors. The Wilder licked his finger and ran it along the joint between door and wall, before examining the result. Then he sniffed around the door handle, which was made of Violet crystal and golden metal. He did this at all four doors, running between them, before pointing at the door on the eastern side.

"What?" asked Tal. "How can he tell?"

"Dust," replied Milla. "Or the lack of it. And a hand leaves oil or sweat on metal. Come on!"

"But he couldn't smell that," said Tal. "Could he?"

Milla didn't answer. She ran towards the door and stood off to one side, the Talon ready. Odris glided over to the other side, Adras next to her.

Jarek tried the door handle. It didn't turn, even when the huge Icecarl began to exert his full strength.

"The Keystone!" snapped Ebbitt. "Use your head, Tal. We can't wait around for you to get on with it!"

Tal flushed and raised the Keystone, directing a beam of Violet at the door handle. It was reflected back, and suddenly the handle turned under Jarek's hand and he thrust it open.

The Wilder sprang through, drawing his chain as he ran. Milla followed him, the Talon extending, followed by the Spiritshadows and Tal and Crow, with Ebbitt and Malen behind.

All of them expected some sort of trap, or enemy left behind by Sushin. But they didn't expect to see a gigantic insect, an awful thin-bodied creature at least fifty stretches long, with hundreds of segmented legs, serrated mandibles longer than Jarek and two huge multifaceted eyes.

Light flared in Sunstones, the Talon extended into a whip of light and Jarek whirled his chain above his head.

Then everyone stopped. The light faded. Milla let her hand drop to her side, and Jarek's chain slowed its terrifying whirl and came to what would be a bruising stop on anyone's side but his own.

The giant insect was dead. Or had never been alive. As they moved forward, Tal saw that it was actually a machine of some kind. It was made of something like the golden metal, though this material had a greenish sheen on the gold. And the great multifaceted eyes were actually made up of hundreds of Sunstones. Dead Sunstones.

It had a sort of saddle high on its back, behind the head with its terrifying mandibles, and the two closest legs had blunt bristles that could be used like rungs on a ladder, where all the other legs had razorlike protrusions.

"A war beast," said Milla in awe. This would be a

terrible foe. It was thin enough to slip through anywhere a human could stand upright, but those mandibles could cut a warrior in two and the legs slice a hundred foes into pieces.

"A Wormwalker," said Ebbitt. "Fascinating. I always thought they were made up."

"They?" asked Crow. "There are more of them?"

"According to the stories, at least a score," said Ebbitt happily. He produced a measuring tape from one of his ample pockets and stretched it between the Wormwalker's mandibles.

"Not now, Great-uncle," said Tal firmly, taking the old man by the elbow. "We're in a hurry, remember?"

They walked quickly past the Wormwalker, careful to keep away from its sharp legs. The insect machine was actually positioned along a curving corridor and, as they rounded the bend, they saw another war machine. Only this Wormwalker was posed differently, its head and part of the body behind reared up, as if it were about to strike down an enemy.

It appeared as dead and frozen as the first one,

but everyone slowed down again except Jarek, and even he circled the head warily and kept his chain at the ready.

"I wonder how many Sunstones you'd need for each one of these," Tal wondered as they passed. There was a third Wormwalker ahead, like the last, reared up in an aggressive attitude.

Ebbitt looked at something under his breastplate and answered absently.

"Seven hundred of at least strength-eighty stones in each eye for full operation. They have not been used since the time of Ramellan and the Shadow Wars."

His Spiritshadow had to nudge him aside from the Wormwalker's legs as he spoke. It was finally clear that he was reading something, something he had stuffed down the front of his robe, against his chest. It wasn't just a weird new habit he'd chosen to annoy Tal.

Tal had a good idea what Ebbitt had concealed there, though he couldn't work out how the old man was carrying it when it weighed as much as he did.

Ebbitt caught Tal's frown, looked down inside his robe again and coughed.

"I was going to tell you," he said. "But it slipped my mind."

"I thought it couldn't change its weight," complained Tal. "It nearly dislocated my arm before!"

"It can't do some alterations itself; you have to ask it the right way," said Ebbitt. "Fortunately I have researched some of the phrases for commanding its obedience. Though not all, by any means, and it is a tricky bit of... of whatever it is..."

"Milla!" Tal called out, for he and Ebbitt had slipped a little way behind. "Ebbitt has the Codex!"

Milla turned back to look, but Jarek continued on past her. As the Wilder walked on towards the third Wormwalker, Tal saw a sudden glint appear in its eye – and multiply like fire across a pool of oil.

20

"Look out!" screamed Tal, but even as the words left his mouth the Wormwalker struck. Its mandibles snapped down at Jarek, gripping the Wilder around the waist. He dropped his chain and his mighty arms pushed against the creature's jaws, trying to keep them apart. Anyone else's hands would have been sliced through, but Jarek's strange skin resisted the mechanical insect's serrated mandibles. Even so, strong as he was, it was clear the Icecarl would soon be crushed.

Tal immediately raised his Sunstone and fired off a Red Ray of Destruction, only to see it absorbed by the Sunstones in the Wormwalker's eye. Adras and Odris flew forward, but as they tried to grip the creature's mandibles to help Jarek, they found themselves repelled by the green sheen on its surface, which was now sparking – another Sunstone-powered effect.

Milla attacked too, whipping a light rope around the Wormwalker's head. But just as the Spiritshadows could not touch the metal, the rope of light was repelled.

Crow threw a knife at one eye, and was gratified and surprised to see a few Sunstones fall out, but not enough to make a difference.

Jarek roared, the Spiritshadows boomed and shouted, Milla cried a war cry and Ebbitt said something to Tal as he fired another Red Ray, this time aiming at the thing's front set of legs.

"What?" shouted Tal. Ebbitt was bobbing around at his side and muttering while trying to read something from the Codex he had under his breastplate.

"The top of its head!" shouted Ebbitt. "In front of… in front of the saddle. You have to pull its… er… brain out."

Tal looked at the Wormwalker, which was shaking Jarek back and forth, its long body undulating wildly behind it all along the corridor. Milla was dancing about in front of it, whipping the light rope from her Talon across its eyes. With every third or fourth stroke, a Sunstone would fail to resist and explode, but there were too many for that tactic to work.

"In front of the saddle?" asked Tal quickly.

"Yes!"

Tal sized up the Wormwalker's motion and started to run. As he ran, he shouted to Adras. "Adras! Adras! Throw me on to the thing's head!"

Adras turned at his voice, but didn't seem to understand. Tal had a momentary vision of the Spiritshadow simply stepping aside to let him slide under the Wormwalker and into the forest of its razor-sharp legs.

"Throw me!" he screamed. "On to its head!"

The Spiritshadow finally got it. He cupped his hands a second before Tal reached him. The Chosen boy leaped, had his feet caught for an instant and was thrown through the air, over the mandibles and the still-struggling Jarek.

He came down hard on the Wormwalker's head and started to slide off, the wrong side, down to the sharp legs. But the saddle was only a handsbreadth away, and he managed to stretch himself to what he was sure was much more than his usual height and grip on to it.

A moment later he had spun around and was in the saddle, holding on desperately as the Wormwalker arched, undulated and shook in an effort to dislodge him.

Tal held on to a ring just in front of the saddle with one hand and clawed at a round panel set in the thing's head, which was the only possible clue to where its brain might be. All his nails broke, but he managed to flip it open. Underneath there was a single Sunstone set in the top of what looked like a crystal cylinder or tube full of a pulsing green fluid.

Tal forced his fingers into the receptacle and tried to pull the cylinder out. But he couldn't get a grip, and he was nearly thrown out of the saddle as the Wormwalker redoubled its efforts to shake him off. It was gyrating up and down from the floor and smacking itself against the ceiling, so that Tal had to fling himself right down on the saddle to avoid being crushed.

"Do… thing imp… !" shouted Ebbitt, his voice only just audible above the din. Tal took a second to translate this in his head as, "Do something imperial!"

Tal grimaced, concentrated and fired a pulse of pure Violet at the Sunstone atop the cylinder. It answered with a flash and the cylinder popped half out of the receptacle. Tal grabbed it, pulled it the rest of the way out and flung it over the side.

He almost went over himself as the Wormwalker froze in mid-undulation. His hand, already sore from the climb up the slopdown, was burning and bleeding again, and he had the familiar feeling of a nearly dislocated shoulder.

Climbing down, he found Ebbitt examining the long crystal tube. It was full of green lumps of something disgusting-looking, floating in what could be cooking oil, but almost certainly wasn't.

"Well done," said Ebbitt, sliding the tube

through his belt. "Very considerate of you to get one of these for me."

Tal shook his head. "I hope there aren't any more Wormwalkers ahead of us," he said. "Ebbitt, can you ask the Codex where Sushin is? It must have taken him quite a while to get this thing going again, so maybe he isn't too far ahead."

Ebbitt nodded, which to Tal meant yes, as he ducked under the Wormwalker's head to where Milla, Crow and Malen were standing solemnly looking up at the body of Jarek.

One look told Tal that somewhere in those last few seconds of struggle, Jarek's strength had failed him and the mandibles had closed.

"The fury did not come to him," said Milla.

"He did not want to live after Kirr was slain," said Malen. "So it is with all Wilders. The fury only fails them when they do not need it any more."

"I was too slow," said Tal. He looked away. "Too slow again..."

"You fought well," said Milla to Tal. "Almost like a Far-Raider. But we have all been too slow. We must not let Sushin have any more time to bring foes like this to life again."

"The Codex can't tell where Sushin is," said Ebbitt, appearing from under the Wormwalker, his breastplate pushed well away from his chest, a strange light now clearly visible shining through his rather grimy undershirt. "A power opposes it."

"What about the Veil?" asked Tal urgently. "Is the Veil still working?"

Ebbitt looked down and muttered a question.

"It's hard to read upside down," he complained. "But the Codex is not to be trusted if I keep it anywhere else, so—"

"The Veil, Ebbitt!"

"It's still up," replied Ebbitt with a smile. Then the smile disappeared, instantly wiped away. "But not for long. The Codex reports the Chamber of the Veil is in use. The Veil is being 'shut down', whatever that is. Three of the Towers are already out, from Violet to Blue. Oh no! Green is going!"

"Where is the Chamber of the Veil?" snapped Tal. "How do we get there?"

Ebbitt looked down, growled in exasperation

and ripped off his crystal breastplate, sending it clattering to the floor. There, tucked into his shirt, was the Codex of the Chosen, or a miniature version of it. A rectangle of pure crystal, its surface shimmered like the reflection of the moon on water.

Ebbitt pulled the Codex out, tearing his shirt, and set it against the wall. Its edges shimmered and then it slowly spread both sideways and up. In a few seconds it was the size Tal remembered, about as tall as Ebbitt and three times as wide.

"How do we get to the Chamber of the Veil from here?" asked Tal. He knew the Codex only answered direct questions.

Dark lines appeared on its surface. A map, with far too much detail for Tal to quickly take in. But there was also a line of text beneath the map, written in Chosen script and Icecarl runes.

Only one way, follow this spiral corridor to the top of the Seventh Tower.

21

"How long will it be until the Veil is completely... ah... shut down?" asked Tal almost before he absorbed the answer to his previous question.

Twenty-nine minutes at current speed of procedure, answered the Codex, again in Chosen script and Icecarl runes, presumably so Milla and Malen could read the answer as well.

"Come on!" shouted Tal. He spun round and started running. From the map, there were at least three thousand stretches of spiralling corridor to run up. It should be possible to make it in under twenty minutes. Provided they didn't run into more Wormwalkers or other obstacles...

Milla, Crow, Malen, Adras and Odris followed Tal without question. Ebbitt coughed and leaned against the wall.

"I'll catch you up," he shouted after them.

When he looked back, the Codex was shrinking and losing its form, becoming a stream of jellylike fluid that was climbing up the wall. Ebbitt pounced upon it and wrestled it back against his chest before starting off after the others at a quick walk.

The corridor wound past several more Wormwalkers, fortunately none of them operational. Tal tried not to slow as he approached each one, though it was hard not to. Instead he called Adras to come close to him, ready to throw him up on to its head if it proved necessary. Milla came close to him too, with Odris at her side, obviously to mimic his tactic if required.

Crow and Malen ran together a little way behind. Tal had stopped worrying about the Freefolk boy. Either he had reformed completely, or he was not prepared to jeopardise his relationship – and his people's – with the Icecarls by doing anything to Tal.

The corridor narrowed a bit after the next turn,

and there were many doors coming off it, one every twenty stretches or so on both sides. The doors were transparent and, as they got close enough, Tal looked left and Milla looked right, in unspoken agreement.

They saw strange things through the doors, but could not stop to look at them. There were many odd-looking machines, of metal and crystal and Sunstones, some of the latter still twinkling and glowing. There was room after room full of animals suspended in clear containers of fluid, animals that Milla recognised as being denizens of the Ice, or distant ancestors of them. There were things like newborn Selski, but not quite the same; and Merwins with no horns; and Wreska only a tenth of the size she knew; and Wrack hounds with strange skin instead of fur; and even shiny Norrworms, no larger than her finger and bundled up in balls of many worms, unlike the huge ones of the distant Ice that denned in pairs.

Onward and upward they ran, the spiralling corridor narrowing with every turn, and the doors showing glimpses of stranger and stranger secrets.

"Ebbitt," panted Tal, "will never get past all this.

He'll open a door and forget what he was doing."

"We should have brought the Codex," said Milla. She was not really panting, but it took an effort to speak normally.

"No time to make it shrink," gasped Tal. "Besides, we know where Sushin must be."

Around another turn, Crow suddenly cried out behind them, and half fell, half stumbled against the wall and immediately threw up. Malen stopped too.

"Too much exertion, too soon," she said, feeling his forehead with her palm. "You must rest for a little while."

"Follow when you can!" shouted Milla, without stopping.

"So, it's just you and me again," said Tal as Milla increased the pace.

"And us!" interrupted Odris. "Why do you always forget us, Tal?"

"He's the Emperor now," said Adras gloomily. "Treats me like a servant."

"I do not!" protested Tal.

"Do too!"

"Save your breath," warned Milla. "It's getting steeper."

The spiral corridor was also winding itself tighter and there were no more doors. It was like running up a very steep hill.

Tal started finding it harder to breathe and a stitch began to grow in his side. He pushed his fist into it and ignored the pain. What was a stitch when the Veil was disappearing with every—

Then he saw it up ahead. The Veil. The corridor ended in absolute, clearly defined darkness.

"Is that... ?" asked Milla as they slowed down.

"Yes, the Veil," said Tal. "Adras and Odris, hold on to each other and on to us. Milla, take my hand. We should go through at a walk and I'll keep my hand on the inside wall."

All four of them joined hands and Tal reached out to touch the inner wall.

"What if there is a trap inside?" asked Milla suspiciously.

Tal shook his head.

"I don't think you can do anything inside the Veil. It not only takes the light away, but breath as well.

It's strange. It is not somewhere you could stay in long enough to set a trap."

Tal took a deep breath, Milla following suit. Then the two of them, and their Spiritshadows, plunged into total darkness.

All sound disappeared with the light. Even the touch of Milla's hand seemed distant and far away to Tal. He could feel the rasp of the stone under his other hand, but it was lessened too. It would be easy to lose one's way in the Veil, to get turned around and blunder about until breath and senses failed.

It was even worse for Milla. She had expected the darkness of the Ice, but this was different. It was not cold, but somehow it leeched both energy and heat out of her and made her shiver, something she rarely did from a simple chill. It also stretched on and on for much longer than Tal had said it would. She could feel his hand, but not the Spiritshadows', and even his hand felt strange and inhuman. The Veil was robbing her of breath and she was sure she would never see the light again—

When they burst out of the Veil, out into the

Sunstone-lit corridor winding its way up and around ahead of them, Milla gasped in relief and swiftly looked at Tal to hide the small sign of her weakness. But Tal was gasping too and did not notice.

"That was bad," said Odris. "I do not think I would go through alone."

"I've been through three times," said Adras proudly.

"Let's hope it's still there when we come back," said Tal grimly. He broke into a run again, the stitch coming back straightaway.

"Will Crow and Malen make it through?" asked Milla.

"Crow's done it before," said Tal, though it took him a few seconds to get breath enough to answer. "He can help Malen. Or they could wait for Ebbitt, I guess."

Tal looked at his Sunstone, to check the time.

"Fourteen minutes gone," he said. "But we must be more than halfway."

They started to run again. Above the Veil there were no more transparent doors, though there were side entrances every now and then, blocked by solid portals of metal or some material that might be wood.

Tal's stitch got worse, twisting deeper into his side. Finally he had to stop and bend over, almost retching from the exertion.

"I will go on," called Milla, but Tal reached out and grabbed her sleeve.

"No," he gasped. "Sushin is too powerful… and if Sharrakor is there… Adras, please, can you carry me?"

"See, he thinks I'm a servant," grumbled Adras.

"I said please," Tal coughed out.

"He did say please," confirmed Odris. "Shall I carry you as well, Milla?"

Milla frowned for a moment, then nodded.

"Yes," she said. "We should have thought of it before. The corridor is high enough and it will be faster."

"I can't go too fast," said Odris. From the tone of her voice she already regretted her offer. "I get tired as well, you know."

Milla and Tal held up their arms and felt the cool

shadowflesh ripple across their wrists as the Spiritshadows gripped them. Adras and Odris were strong in the full, clear light of the corridor, and they lifted the Chosen and Icecarl with ease, and quickly accelerated up and around the bend.

It was much faster than the two humans could have run, though Adras had a tendency to cut corners and smack Tal into the side of the corridor, and Odris dipped every ten stretches or so and dragged Milla's feet along the ground.

After at least twenty more turns around the steadily steepening spiral corridor, Tal was dizzy. His stitch had gone, but he felt just as bad from the dizziness. If they kept going he would be in no state to face Sushin. He wouldn't even be able to see straight, let alone do any Light Magic.

"Stop!" he called. "We must be close!"

The Spiritshadows slowed to a halt and let go of their passengers. Tal staggered around for a few seconds, shaking his head until the dizziness passed.

"It can't be much further," Tal said again. He consulted his Sunstone. "Nineteen minutes. We have ten minutes until the Veil is gone."

"We should make a plan," said Milla. "What if Sushin has free Spiritshadows with him?"

Tal nodded. He had seen many free shadows in the Red Tower, above the Veil, brought across from Aenir to be the vanguard of an even larger force that would follow when the Veil fell.

"I think we have to concentrate on Sushin," he said. "Strike at him, as he's the one who can use the Violet Keystone. Adras and Odris can try to keep the free shadows off our backs."

"I cannot offer any better plan," said Milla. "We must hope fate favours us, and be bold and brave."

She held out her hand and turned her wrist up, showing the scars of her oaths.

"We have many vows between us, Tal," she said. "Let us add one more, without blood, for there is no time. Let us go together to save our world."

Tal held out his wrist, similarly scarred, and held it against Milla's.

"Together, to save the world. We will defeat Sushin and Sharrakor!"

Tal met Milla's eyes for a full second and both of

them saw something of themselves in the other's eyes. Somehow the Chosen had become almost an Icecarl, and the Icecarl was almost a Chosen. Emperor and War-Chief, both of them blending the best of their two peoples.

Then they broke apart and started off up the corridor, with their Spiritshadows behind. Two people of the Dark World, striding out together to face their enemy, the enemy of all life under the Veil.

The Chamber of the Veil was similar to the room at the top of the Red Tower, only larger and more impressive. It had four wide, arched windows that looked out to blue sky and sunshine. The floor was not checkered, but set with tiny Sunstones that shone with soft violet light which mixed with the golden sunshine.

Tal and Milla came to it sooner than they expected, the corridor simply turning steeply and merging into the floor of the chamber. They ducked down as they saw the edge, then peered up over the lip of the ramp.

There was no tree of bells as in the Red Tower,

Tal saw, but there was a somewhat similar pyramid-shaped plinth in the centre of the chamber. Parts of it shone like a Sunstone, in distinct colours. With a shock, Tal realised that the entire plinth was actually carved out of an enormous Sunstone, one that must have had a diameter of three stretches or more. He didn't know you could carve a Sunstone into any shape – let alone a pyramid.

As Tal watched, the horizontal band of yellow light in the pyramid went dark, and he saw with a feeling of terror that this was a progressive darkness, and that more than half of this enormous Sunstone had ceased to shine. Five distinct bands were dark, from the base of the pyramid up, and only two still shone. Orange and Red.

Then Tal saw Sushin. The bloated Chosen was on the far side of the pyramid, holding the Violet Keystone in his hand. He was sending pulses of Violet into the pyramid, pulses that Tal instinctively knew were closing – no, what was the term the Codex had used? *Shutting down the Veil.*

Sushin's Spiritshadow, a monster of spikes, with

four hooked claws and two massive horns sprouting from its head, loomed up behind its master. But there were no other Spiritshadows in the chamber, at least that Tal could see. He felt a rising hope build inside him. Sushin was a dangerous enemy, but he was alone.

"Attack on three?" he whispered to Milla, and she nodded. Tal saw that the Talon on her hand was already glowing as she held it out from her body.

Tal held up three fingers. Closed one, his heart pounding. Closed two, his heart going faster than it ever had before, red light pulsing in his Sunstone. Closed three—

"Go!"

Everything happened too quickly then. There was no time for thought, only instinct.

Tal jumped forward and fired a Red Ray at the Spiritshadow, because Sushin was protected by too many Sunstones. It hit the thing between the eyes and it reeled back, clasping its head with two hooked hands.

Milla charged straight at Sushin, the Talon fully extended, a long lash of light twisting and curling from it as if it had a life of its own.

Sushin didn't move. He stood there like a statue, the Violet Keystone on his finger continuing to pulse at the pyramid stone.

The Orange band of light went out. Sushin's Spiritshadow dashed forward, only to be met by another Red Ray from Tal as he advanced. Adras and Odris zoomed ahead, to grab the enemy Spiritshadow.

Milla struck at Sushin with the Talon, and Sunstones flared on every hem of his violet-coloured robe. The lash of light from the Talon was deflected, whipping back over Milla's head. Without a second thought, the Icecarl flipped a bone knife out of her sleeve and tried to stab Sushin with a more physical weapon. But the Sunstones flared red and the knife was burned away in an incandescent flash.

Milla howled in fury and tried to punch the Talon into Sushin's face. More Sunstones flared, this time blue and green, and she found herself picked up by some unseen force and thrown over the Chosen's head. Somersaulting in the air, she landed on her toes and rushed back, as Tal ran forward to join her, half his mind focused on forming the beginnings of the Violet Unravelling in his Sunstone.

Milla struck again first, and was once more thrown aside by Sushin's defensive spells, sliding across the floor with an angry scream. On the other side of the chamber, Adras and Odris were twisting the Spiritshadow's claws behind its back and holding it so it couldn't use its horns or teeth. Then they proceeded to tear it apart, bellowing and thundering with every wrench.

"Stay clear!" shouted Tal. A Violet cloud was spewing out of his half of the Violet Keystone. With a flick of his wrist, he sent it spinning into Sushin.

Every Sunstone on Sushin burst into brilliance as the Violet Unravelling hit. For a moment it looked like they might resist it, or even turn it back. Then they started to explode, one by one, as the Unravelling bit into them.

Yet Sushin still didn't move, keeping his half of the Violet Keystone on the pyramid. Even as his last Sunstone vaporised and the Unravelling started to eat away at his clothes and exposed flesh, he did not look away or lower his hand.

Then the last band of colour in the pyramid went out. All seven bands were dark.

Sushin moved swift as a cavernmouth, turning his part of the Keystone back to bathe himself in Violet light of a different shade from the Unravelling. They cancelled each other out, in the very second that Tal and Milla attacked again.

Tal's Red Ray was the strongest he'd ever dared, a finger-thin beam of vicious light aimed directly at Sushin's head. But Sushin caught it on his Keystone, deflecting most of it to the ceiling, though his hand was burned.

Milla came in low, sweeping the lash of light from the Talon across Sushin's legs. With inhuman speed, Sushin countered with a shield of Violet, but he was not quite fast enough and the lash cut deeply into his legs, just above his ankles.

As before, when Milla had thrown her Merwin-horn sword at him, no blood came out of these wounds. But Sushin did fall to the ground, his hamstrings cut. He wriggled like a Wormwalker around the pyramid, shrieking as he scuttled. "No, it's not me! It's not me! Don't kill Sushin!"

Then another voice came from somewhere inside him, a deeper, stranger voice, louder and more horrible than anything that came from any human mouth.

"You have lost! The Veil is destroyed! The time of Sharrakor has come!"

Then it spoke a quick series of words, words that neither Tal nor Milla knew, but somehow still recognised.

"Nvarth! Ghesh gheshthil lurese!"

Then it spoke words they did know, words that hit them like physical blows.

"Adras eris Aenir! Odris eris Aenir!"

With those words, Adras and Odris disappeared. To Tal and Milla it was like having something torn out of their bodies, a pain so terrible that both of them were instantly felled, toppling to the floor like chopped trees.

Through a haze of crippling pain, Tal saw Sushin crawling back around the pyramid, crawling towards him. He tried to focus on his Sunstone, but everything was blurry and he could not make his hand do what he wanted.

Milla tried too, and actually managed to drag herself closer to Tal and raise her hand with the Talon. But no light whip came and she could not keep going. All her strength was gone.

They were dying, Tal realised, though he could not think clearly for the pain. This was what had happened to Ethar and the other Chosen outside the Audience Chamber. Sushin – or whatever was *in* Sushin – had sent their Spiritshadows back to Aenir and the sudden shock had killed them.

"I shall take that," said Sushin in his normal voice as he crawled up next to Tal. One blubbery hand reached across and slid the Violet Keystone from Tal's finger. The Chosen boy tried to resist, but it was no good. His arm just flopped and the pain stabbed through his eyes into his brain. "I think this is best put back together."

Sushin sat up and inspected the half Keystone he had taken. But before he could slip it on his own finger next to the half he already had, a beam of intense red light shot out and struck him full on the hand. The Keystone ring fell to the floor and bounced away.

The voice inside Sushin growled then, a sound that drove fear even through the pain in Tal.

Another Red Ray struck Sushin in the chest, smoke curling up as it drilled a hole right through him. He growled again and struggled to get to his feet, forgetting his hamstrings and bulk. He fell over again and started to slither along the ground like a snake or worm, towards the pyramid.

Through the deep cuts and rents in the Chosen's robe, Tal saw not flesh and blood, but shadow.

Tal rolled over, crying with the pain, and saw Crow standing near the entrance. The Freefolk boy was holding out his Sunstone in the approved manner taught in the Lectorium, his face wrinkled in concentration. Red light bathed his hand, growing in intensity as he prepared another Red Ray. A second later it shot out, striking sparks as it cut through some metal on Sushin's robes.

But it still did not slow whatever Sushin was. He reached the pyramid and dragged himself up, using it as a prop so he could aim his Sunstone at Crow.

"Not! Not a man!" screamed Tal, the words interspersed with sobs. "A shadow! Malen…"

He could say no more, his strength exhausted.

23

As Tal's words echoed in the chamber, Sushin fired a globe of shimmering Violet back at Crow, and Malen's voice filled the air. A quavering, uncertain voice, speaking the words of the Prayer to Asteyr.

Crow dived aside and the Violet globe sailed past him, struck the wall between two windows and exploded straight through, out into the air beyond, followed by a great plume of stone chips and dust.

The effect of Malen's voice was equally spectacular. Sushin froze, his mouth open, his hand extended. Then his whole body blurred. There was his human form, and then there was a dark double that was separating out of him, stepping back from the human version.

It was a shadow leaving the flesh it had hidden in. As it came out, it changed and grew, growing larger and more menacing. Slowly it assumed the shape that only Tal had seen before.

A monster. A dragon. Sharrakor himself.

Fully out of his fleshly host, his reptilian body stretched from floor to ceiling. His head was long and spiked, his many-toothed mouth big enough to snap up Tal in a single bite. His wings were furled, as they would not fit in the chamber. His tail was long and ended in a bone shaped like a butcher's cleaver.

"Asteyr herself could not bind me alone," roared Sharrakor. "How could you succeed where she failed and died for her failure? I do not see Danir, Susir and Grettir come to do her work!"

The shadowdragon's voice momentarily drowned out Malen's and for a moment Tal thought she had stopped. But then her voice came back again. Quiet, slow, but unafraid. Whether her prayer could bind Sharrakor or not, he clearly didn't like it.

"Speak your spell!" he roared again. "I shall not stay to hear it. But you I shall seek out, witch of the Ice, if you still live when I return. Go now and tell your peoples that the Veil is destroyed! That Sharrakor will soon finish the war your ancestors so foolishly began!"

With that, the shadowdragon's head flashed down and bit off Sushin's hand. It held it in its mighty jaws for an instant, then the Spiritshadow disappeared and the hand fell to the floor – minus the Sunstone ring that had been there a moment before.

Malen kept reciting the Prayer to Asteyr, even though the object of it was no longer visible. Crow rushed over to where Tal and Milla were writhing on the ground.

"What happened?" he asked. "Where are you hurt?"

"Spiritshadows," said Tal. He could barely speak between sobs of pain. "Sent back. Aenir. We... must... follow. Get Ebbitt. Get ring. Please... please..."

Tal watched Crow turn and pick up the ring. This

is where it happens, his shocked brain thought. This is the betrayal. This is where Crow takes the ring and walks away. There, he is turning now. This is the end—

He was still thinking that when Crow slipped the half Keystone back on his finger.

"I know the Way to Aenir," said Crow. "Ebbitt showed me once. But I never went. Now seems the time."

"Get Milla," whispered Tal. He couldn't concentrate. "You... reflect the light into our stones..."

Milla had already crawled a little closer. She did not speak or make any sound of pain when Crow grabbed her and dragged her next to Tal, rolling them both on to their backs and resting their Sunstones on their chests, their heads on his lap.

"Milla," muttered Tal. "Watch... Sunstone... follow... repeat..."

Crow began to visualise the colours and speak the Way to Aenir. His Sunstone flashed and he directed beams from it to the Sunstones clasped in Milla's and Tal's hands.

Through the pain, Tal tried to repeat the words Crow was speaking. He knew that they must get to Aenir. They had to find Adras and Odris, who must be dying there. They had to get back and repair or raise the Veil again, and prepare for Sharrakor's invasion...

Milla followed the words without thinking of anything else. The words and colours were all that mattered. She had to survive. Her people were depending upon her. She had failed them already and had not defended the Veil. She must live to reverse her defeat...

Malen finished the Prayer to Asteyr. But she did not feel its success. Sharrakor must have returned to Aenir to avoid the spell. He was not lurking, somehow invisible.

Malen saw Crow sitting with Tal and Milla cradled against him, with waves of many-coloured light washing across all three of them. She saw Sushin dead or dying next to the pyramid, blood flowing freely now that the shadow in him was gone.

Then she saw a flash of light at the very apex of

the pyramid. It had been completely dark, but now the top began to shine with a weak red light. Malen watched it, thinking the light might spread, but it didn't. Only the top glowed.

She heard a noise behind her and whirled round, suddenly afraid. She was effectively alone, a Crone disconnected from her mothers and sisters, without Shield Maidens or hunters to protect her.

It was Ebbitt, puffing and straining as he climbed the ramp. He saw Malen staring at him, wild-eyed, and Sushin behind, the almost totally dark pyramid, and the rainbow-cocooned trio of Crow, Tal and Milla.

"What happened?"

Malen shivered and found herself unable to speak, the words caught in her throat. Ebbitt rushed past her, and after a further glance at the three who had clearly gone to Aenir, he knelt beside Sushin, his Sunstone glowing as he called up healing magic. Ebbitt's Spiritshadow sniffed at Sushin, then wandered over to sniff at the point where Adras and Odris had pulled apart Sushin's spiky Spiritshadow.

"He... he had a shadow in him," blurted out Malen. "Sharrakor. A dragon. He made Adras and Odris disappear, and Tal and Milla fell down. We were watching and Crow used Light Magic and I tried the Prayer of Asteyr, but Sharrakor said the Veil was destroyed and he'd come back..."

"The Veil isn't destroyed, it's just fraying at the edges," said Ebbitt sharply. There was no indication of his usual dodderiness. "The Red Keystone is keeping it going, at least for a while. Though not as strongly as it should, perhaps. What did Sharrakor say about coming back?"

"He said he'd come back and finish the war," said Malen. "Oh, I'd better... I'd better report..."

She stood up straighter and put her hands to her head. But the more she tried to reach the other Crones, the more she heard Sharrakor's awful voice, and his threat that he would find her...

"That'll hold you," said Ebbitt.

Sushin opened his eyes. "Thank you but that will be quite..." His voice trailed off and an expression of total bewilderment spread across his face. "Where am I? Who are you?"

"Rest now," soothed Ebbitt. "You've had an accident."

"I was in Aenir," said Sushin. "Having breakfast with Julper Yen-Baren. He was going to help me climb to Yellow…"

He paused for a moment.

"I dreamed," he said after the pause. "A terrible dream. My head was opened and a stranger poured himself inside—"

His voice was getting more and more shrill as he spoke, building towards hysteria. Ebbitt hastily raised his Sunstone and a green light fell down on Sushin's face. The Chosen's eyes closed and he slumped back against the pyramid.

"I'm not sure whether it will be more merciful to help him live or die," remarked Ebbitt. "I suppose, as in so many things, fate will decide. Imagine his last memory being breakfast with Julper Yen-Baren! More than thirty years ago. I bet it was a rotten breakfast too. Julper was a mean fellow. Come on then."

"Come on?" asked Malen. "Where?"

"Aenir," said Ebbitt impatiently. "You'll have to

share my Sunstone for the transition. Just stare at it and repeat what I say."

"Aenir!" exclaimed Malen. "I can't go there!"

"You'll be needed," said Ebbitt. "From what I read in the Codex."

"What do you mean?"

"Ah, that would be telling," replied Ebbitt.

"Yes it would!" said Malen, stamping her foot. "So tell me, you... you old hoarder!"

Being called a hoarder was a serious insult among Icecarls, for sharing food and essentials was a central part of any clan's survival. Ebbitt, however, was not offended.

"Oh, put like that, I suppose," he said, rubbing his nose. "Having got rid of the Veil, or close enough, Sharrakor's next step must be to undo the Forgetting. Since it was your Crones – or the historical equivalent – that did the Forgetting in the first place, it seems to me that you'll be required."

"But I'm only a young Crone," protested Malen.

"You're the *only* Crone who's right here right now," answered Ebbitt, taking her arm. "Just stare into this Sunstone."

"But I should inform—"

"No time for that!" cried Ebbitt. His Spiritshadow had sidled up to his side and his Sunstone was already changing colour, beginning the sequence that was part of the Way to Aenir. "They'll figure it out. Remember, say the words after me!"

He started reciting, and Malen, despite herself, stared into the Sunstone and repeated the words. Aenir! She was going to Aenir, where no Icecarl save Milla had been for a thousand circlings or more!

Neither of them noticed a trickle of silver slide out the back of Ebbitt's shirt and roll across the floor. The Codex of the Chosen had spent too long in Aenir and it had no plans to return.

Tal, Milla and Crow fell on to a stone platform that wriggled under them and tried to crawl away. The weaker sunshine of Aenir fell upon their changed bodies, the Aeniran versions of themselves. They were a little shorter and slimmer, and their skin glowed with a slight lustre.

The pain was still with Tal and Milla, but to a much lesser extent. Tal could feel Adras somewhere. Too far away, but not totally absent. So the Storm Shepherd was still alive, thank the Light.

Tal sat up and looked around. They didn't seem to be in immediate danger, though the stone slab moving under him was a bit creepy. It was not the only apparently solid object that was moving. The remains of a nearby wall were also slowly shifting away, trailing old mortar.

"Ruins," said Crow. He was standing up, shaking his head a little as he looked around him and down at his changed self. "So this is Aenir. I always wanted to see this."

"Can you see any enemies?" asked Milla. She stood up too, then sat down again rather too quickly and began massaging her legs and doing exercises with her arms.

"No," replied Crow. "At least I don't think so. There are a lot of stones moving around. Very slowly. Where are we anyway?"

"A ruined city," said Tal, which was pretty obvious to everyone. At least that was what it looked like. You never could be too sure in Aenir what anything really was, as opposed to what it seemed to be. Certainly they were surrounded by many ruined buildings, and there were plenty more as far as he could see, rising up into the hills around.

"What happened?" asked Milla. "I felt Odris...

wrenched… away. It was worse than when the Merwin gored me."

Tal shook his head.

"I'm not sure. Somehow Sharrakor sent them back here. But they're coming. I think."

"Yes," confirmed Milla. "I can feel Odris getting closer. But they are far away."

"We failed," said Tal, after they were both silent for a moment. "The Veil is gone."

"The Ice will melt," said Milla quietly. "The Slepenish and the Selski will die, and my people with them."

"And any who do survive will be slain by the shadows Sharrakor will lead back there."

"Not if we stop him," said Milla. "Perhaps we can do this one small thing, when we have failed in so many others."

"We must try," said Tal. He was thinking of his family, back in the Castle. He had saved Graile, there was a good chance his father, Rerem, could be rescued from the Orange Keystone, and Gref and Kusi reunited with them. But for what? So they could all die together when Sharrakor invaded?

"No," Milla contradicted him. "We must *succeed*."

Tal and Crow nodded grimly in agreement. Tal forced himself to his feet. He tottered a little and had to put his hand on Milla's shoulder to balance. Crow offered a steadying hand, but Tal refused it. He managed to stand unassisted and look out in the direction he felt the Storm Shepherds were coming from. Seeing nothing, he slowly turned around in a circle.

There was a speck on the horizon and for a moment Tal thought it was Adras. But it didn't look right and after a second he realised it was flying away. He pointed it out to Milla and Crow.

"What's that?"

Crow looked, but couldn't see it. Milla shaded her eyes with her hand.

"A dragon. Sharrakor," she said, the name sending a thrill of fear through each of them. "He is not dark like a shadow here, but bright as a mirror shining in the sun."

"Watch him as far as you are able," said Tal. "We'll have to follow when we can."

A movement attracted his attention and he

whirled unsteadily. But it was only a boulder crossing between two walls, in a slow and stately progress.

Tal sighed and sat back down. There was nothing they could do for a little while. They had to regain their strength and wait for Adras and Odris to arrive.

But it was not Adras and Odris who arrived. There was a shimmer in the air next to them, and a sudden rainbow. Tal and Milla scurried back, readying Sunstone and Talon. Crow took cover behind the wall and picked up what he hoped was an inanimate rock. His knife had not come across with the transfer, but some of his other odds and ends had, though perhaps not without some transformation.

"Chosen!" snapped Tal. "Coming through from the Castle!"

The rainbow grew brighter, there was a flash, then Ebbitt and Malen were standing in front of them, accompanied by a dark green cat with a light green mane. Ebbitt was clutching his chest, and for a moment Tal thought he was having a heart attack, until the old man stamped his feet and launched into a tirade.

"Dark throttle the thing! Just when we needed it the most!"

"Hello, Great-uncle," said Tal. "What was it you needed?"

"The cursed Codex," shouted Ebbitt, flinging himself face down on the stone to beat at it with his fists. His maned cat sat next to him and started licking its paws. "It got away from me."

"Welcome, Malen," said Milla, clapping her fists. "I am glad you are with us."

Malen was looking around, watching the creeping rocks and shivering walls. She stared back at Milla and belatedly clapped her fists in return.

"Greetings, War-Chief. I wasn't sure, but Ebbitt insisted... I have to help stop Sharrakor from undoing the Forgetting, before the Veil fails."

"What?" snapped Tal. "What do you mean *before the Veil fails*?"

Ebbitt stopped beating at the stone with his fists and rolled on his side. His cat moved aside a little crossly to give him room, then resumed its toilet.

Tal noticed that while its short hair was green, its eyes were yellow and its claws remarkably white.

"Lokar replaced and resealed the Red Keystone," he said. "Or the other way around. Anyway, it will keep the Veil going – at less than full strength – for about seven days, by my calculations."

"Your calculations!" exclaimed Tal.

"The Codex helped me with the hard bit, carrying the decimal point all over the place," admitted Ebbitt. "We talked about it as I was coming up after you hotheads. Always best to plan for the worst, I say."

"Seven days!" exclaimed Tal, and Milla echoed him, as Ebbitt frowned.

"It's not long, but I could be out an hour or two—" Ebbitt started to say. He stopped as Tal and Milla laughed and cheered. Crow smiled briefly, but kept watching the surrounding ruins and the sky.

"Seven days!" Tal exclaimed again. "We thought the Veil was already gone! This gives us… this gives everyone… a chance."

"Yes, it's all quite simple," growled Ebbitt. "Find Sharrakor, stop him from undoing the Forgetting and raising an army of tens of thousands of Aenir-ans, get the other half of the Violet Keystone back, return to the Castle, restore the Veil, settle the war with the Icecarls, free the Underfolk—"

"Yes!" interrupted Crow.

"As I was saying, free the Underfolk and... I've lost my locomotor of thought."

"The Storm Shepherds!" interrupted Crow again, pointing at the sky. "At least, I hope that's what they are."

Tal and Milla turned together and held out their arms. Two huge figures of cloud swooped down and embraced them so vigorously they would have fallen over again if they hadn't been almost crushed in puffy arms. Odris cried as well, rain pouring out in streams from the side of her head, making Ebbitt's cat give a strange yipping cry and jump aside.

"We almost died!" sobbed Odris. "And we ended up back at Hrigga Hill and it tried to eat us!"

"I want to give your shadow back," said Adras. "It hurt too much."

"Yes," said Tal, pushing Adras's arms aside and

stepping back. "I think it is time we undid the binding between us. We should go into the next fight as we mean to go on. Without Spiritshadows or bound companions."

25

"I will be sorry to see the old cat go." Ebbitt sighed. "But I see your point."

"Oh, I didn't mean your—" Tal started to say.

"We've had one rule for some and a different rule for others for too long," said Ebbitt. He leaned over and rubbed his green cat under the chin. It purred and shifted its head so he would scratch the best spots. "Got to set an example for you young folk, don't I? Now, how do we go about it?"

"Um, I don't know," said Tal. "I thought you might."

"Not on the curriculum." Ebbitt sighed again. "Finding and binding, that was it."

"I know," said Malen quietly. "You use a variation of the Prayer to Asteyr to bind them in the first place. I can see it in the Aenirans. I can undo the binding between Tal, Milla and the Storm Shepherds. I don't know about yours, Ebbitt. The... cat... was unwilling originally and the binding is very old and strong."

"Do it then," said Milla. She would get her own shadow back! It was a step towards being a normal Icecarl again, a step she never thought she would be able to take. Yet at the same time, she had become used to Odris, and the Storm Shepherd had been a good and helpful companion. If a trifle annoying at times.

"Stand in a line," ordered Malen tentatively. "Next to one another."

They all shuffled into a line, Ebbitt still scratching the neck of his cat. Tal noticed that there were the beginnings of tears in the old man's eyes, but he didn't say anything. He was sad himself. All his life he had wanted a powerful Spiritshadow, to help him gain a high place in the Castle. But all that was gone. If they survived they would live in new times and there was no place for Aeniran – or human – slaves.

Malen began to chant as they stood silently in front of her. The words were familiar, many of them from what Tal now knew was the Prayer to Asteyr, but with a different cadence and rhythm. He felt the words resonate deep inside his bones, sending a shivery, feverish feeling through every part of his body.

The chant grew faster and stronger, and Malen began to stamp around in a circle, punctuating every ten words or so with a heavier stomp, sending dust flying.

Slowly, in answer to the words, shadows began to creep out of the three Aeniran creatures. Human shadows, which flowed slowly across the stones towards the feet of their original casters.

Malen shouted the last word and came to a sudden stop. Tal felt his shadow reconnect, and the connection he had with Adras was totally severed. For a moment, he felt thick in the head, as if he had a cold. Then he realised that the sense of the wind and the weather that came from Adras was gone.

Tal turned to Adras, and Milla to Odris.

"Well, that's that," said Tal in a small voice. "Thank you for everything you've done for me, Adras."

"I thank you too, Odris," said Milla. "I hope you bear no ill will for the times I have been hard with you. Farewell."

"Farewell?" asked Odris. "We aren't going anywhere without you. Certainly not back to our old life at Hrigga Hill. Far too boring."

"We're going to come and watch you fight Sharrakor," said Adras. "We'll even help if we can, though he is the Overlord and all that."

"The Overlord?" asked Tal. His mind was only half on the conversation, as he was watching Ebbitt kneel down by his cat and bare his neck, as if inviting it to bite him or something. Milla had seen it too, and was already moving across, ready to intervene.

"Sure," said Adras. "The King or whatever. Odris said."

"What?" asked Tal, tensing as the green cat leaned forward and opened its mouth, revealing teeth as white as its claws, but much larger. Would it kill Ebbitt for enslaving it for so long? Milla took another step closer, the Talon extending.

"That's why we had to obey back in the Dark World," said Odris. "Sharrakor holds the oaths of most Aenirans from the old times, including our parents. But we don't have to obey him in everything. At least, I don't think so."

The cat licked Ebbitt's face, making him splutter and almost fall over, and jumped away, a green flash speeding through the ruins.

"That's what my shadowguard did," said Tal.

"He was with me for sixty years," said Ebbitt. He sighed and accepted Milla's help to get up. "Well, we had best be getting on, children."

"Where?" asked Tal. "Where will Sharrakor be? And how does he undo the Forgetting?"

No one answered him. It was clear from the looks on the faces of humans and Storm Shepherds alike that no one knew the answer to his questions.

"I don't know," said Milla. "But I do know someone we can ask."

"Who?"

"Zicka the Kurshken," said Milla. "At Kurshken Corner. Wherever that is."

"Kurshken Corner?" said Odris. "I know how to get there, provided it hasn't moved lately. Assuming this is Rorn, which I guess it must be."

"Rorn?" asked Tal.

"Rorn?" echoed Ebbitt.

Milla and Crow looked at their shocked expressions.

"Rorn is forbidden to the Chosen," explained Tal. "Though I don't know why. We were taught never to go there… come here."

"The penalty is death," said Ebbitt. "I always wanted to take a look myself. This must be it. I know Rorn was a ruined city, heavily staked."

"Staked?" asked Crow.

"Staked through with Sunstone stakes," said Ebbitt. "Like the Chosen Enclave. To stop it from moving around. If we see some of those, then it must be Rorn. I wonder whose city it was and who lived here."

"Sharrakor, of course," said Odris. "Even *I* know that. It was the capital, before the Forgetting. All

Sharrakor's people lived here before they got killed in the war. He's the only one left."

"This was a city of dragons?" asked Milla.

"No, silly," said Odris. "Sharrakor isn't a dragon all the time. He's a doubleganger, or maybe a tripleganger. A shaper. He can turn into two or three different things, big like the dragon, or small like a mind-drill. The really bad ones that climb into your brain. That's what the shapers used to do a lot. That's one of the ways they ruled everyone else in the old times."

"Why didn't you tell us this before?" exclaimed Tal. "It would have been useful to know that Sharrakor could become a... a shadow mind-drill... back in the Castle."

"You never asked," said Odris primly. "And I never heard you mention Sharrakor at all, so it's *your* fault, not mine. And Adras didn't know because he never paid any attention to my lessons."

"Never!" announced Adras proudly. "Too boring."

Tal sighed. If only he had taken Odris with him instead of Adras when they met the Empress and the Light Vizier. If only he had taken Odris with him full stop. But that was an old and familiar feeling by now. Adras was Adras, as Ebbitt was Ebbitt. They both had their advantages, he supposed.

"Let's assume this is Rorn," said Milla, bringing them all back on track. "How far is Kurshken Corner, Odris?"

"Half a day's flight, maybe less," Odris replied with a shrug. "If it hasn't moved."

"Three or four days' walk," mused Milla. "Too long. Is there some way we can all fly?"

"I could carry Tal and someone else," declared Adras. He flexed the muscle in his puffy arms. "I am the strongest!"

"I can only carry Milla," said Odris. "We could leave Ebbitt or Crow behind. Or Malen."

"No," said Crow. "It is my fight too. The Freefolk should be represented."

"We can't leave anyone behind," said Tal. He was thinking as he spoke. Perhaps there was a way to use the Storm Shepherds more effectively. "Ebbitt, what if we made a boat of light and sort of...

crossed it with a Hand of Light. If we could keep it going, it could lift us up and Adras and Odris could push or pull it."

A little of Ebbitt's usual spark returned to his eyes. This was the sort of thing he liked. A crazy idea that most Chosen would refuse to even think about.

"You have half of the Violet Keystone, which is very powerful," he mused. "If we bond the mesh with Violet and weave it Green… Blue traces… yes, yes… What are you waiting for? There's not time to stand around! You start on a backbone of Violet and I'll do the planking in Green with Yellow perhaps…"

Tal smiled. It was a little forced, but still a smile. Then he began to focus on his Sunstone. He and Ebbitt would build a flying boat of light, propelled by Storm Shepherds, to take them to Kurshken Corner and beyond.

Kurshken Corner looked very odd from the air. It was a huge flooded field filled with giant leafy balls of yellow vegetation, a lot like vastly overgrown sprouts, outsized versions of the ones the Underfolk grew in their subterranean greenhouses. Most of the sprouts were the size of a Chosen family's greeting room, but some were much larger. They were clearly inhabited, as Kurshken could be seen coming and going between the different plants, skipping through the shallow water or racing along the many raised levees that crisscrossed the field.

Not that Tal had much time to look. Their flying

boat, modelled on Asteyr's Orskir, required constant attention to stay both airborne and together. It was drawn by the two Storm Shepherds pulling on blue traces, but the actual lifting came from a variation of the Hand of Light spell, and Tal or Ebbitt had to keep it going with constant infusions of power from their Sunstones. Crow and Milla had each helped them from time to time, but were not practised enough to take over completely.

With varying levels of power, the boat flew along at an erratic speed, depending on the Storm Shepherds' way with the winds and their own endurance. There were sometimes quite alarming variations in altitude as the various Sunstone-wielders changed shifts and combinations. The only person who wasn't worried was Malen, who had fallen asleep. The unbinding of the Aenirans had taken its toll and she had not been able to stay awake, much as she wanted to see the strange territory they flew over and the Aeniran denizens they encountered in the air or spotted on the ground.

The arrival of the flying boat at Kurshken Corner

was greeted by the Kurshken with some alarm. There was some alarm on board as well, as the boat lurched and bobbed down to a heavy, skidding landing in a vacant area next to one of the levees. As soon as they were safely down, Tal and Ebbitt made sure Malen was awake and everyone was standing up, then they let the boat of light fade away. The Storm Shepherds, relieved of the blue traces, flitted back to float above the rest of their party.

Before everyone could climb out of the ankle-deep water to the levee, they were surrounded by scores of knee-high green lizards, each of them bearing a bow with a nocked arrow. The arrows had bright blue heads and looked highly poisonous.

"Peace!" called out Milla. "We are friends of Quorr Quorr Quorr Quorr Ahhtorn Sezicka!"

Tal shut his mouth. He'd been about to blurt out the short form "Zicka", which was all he could remember of their friend's name.

The name relieved the tension somewhat. The Kurshken lowered their bows, but did not, Tal noticed, return their arrows to the quivers on their scaly backs. In the rear ranks, he saw several lizards turn and dash away, skipping across the water without actually going through it.

One lizard, who had two huge ivory teeth bound into the shoulders of his woven-grass harness, approached and bowed.

"I am Quorr Quorr Quorr Quorr Quorr Jak-Quorr Jareskk Yazeqicka," the lizard announced, his voice deeper than anyone who had not met a Kurshken before would suspect. "You may call me Yazeq. Four of you I suspect I know from my triple-sister's second-clutch fifth-birthing's report – you know him as Zicka. You I think are Milla, and Tal, and the Storm Shepherds Odris and Adras."

Everyone bowed in return, Adras nearly colliding with Tal's head. Milla confirmed their names, and introduced Ebbitt, Malen and Crow.

"Come," said Yazeq, with a particular glance at Ebbitt. "You must be tired. You may rest in our guest roro, or as you may wish to call it, roroqqolleckechahen."

"I'll say roro," Ebbitt replied weakly. Tal took his arm and looked down at his great-uncle with concern. Since his Spiritshadow had left, Ebbitt seemed older and more tired. The – admittedly rather lunatic – spark in his eyes had dimmed and he looked pale, the Aeniran glow absent from his face. Maintaining the flying boat had also taken far more out of him, Tal saw, than Ebbitt would admit. Tal felt bad about it, for he had taken his great-uncle's power, skill and endurance for granted.

"Are you all right, Ebbitt?" asked Milla.

"I am weary," said Ebbitt. "Very weary indeed. It comes from having to do more than my share of the work, but perhaps Tal will be less lazy in the future."

Tal scowled, but only because it was clear Ebbitt's heart wasn't in the insult. His great-uncle really was tired.

The roro turned out to be one of the huge sprout vegetables. The outer, living leaves concealed a solid husk, which was hollow and had been outfitted most comfortably with rugs and carpets woven from various natural fibres. As it was a guest roro, there also were a number of wooden chairs of different sizes, and drinking horns that varied in length from finger-sized to one as long as Tal's arm.

As they settled down on chairs, on rugs, or in the air and accepted suitably sized drinking horns filled with a sweet juice or sap, the leaves parted to admit another Kurshken. Though all Kurshken looked remarkably similar, something about this one made him instantly known to Tal and Milla.

"Zicka!"

"Indeed," said the lizard. "Welcome to Kurshken Corner, that in our tongue we call—"

Ebbitt interrupted with a fit of sudden coughing. Tal would have been concerned if he hadn't seen the faint glint in his great-uncle's eyes.

"I had not looked to see you so soon," continued Zicka as he sat down and accepted a drink. "But I am glad to see you escaped the Waspwyrm. Did you manage to return the Codex to its rightful place?"

"Sort of," replied Tal, sharing a glance with Milla. "But we have a bigger problem now, one that we hope you can help us with."

Speaking quickly, taking it in turns with Milla and ignoring the occasional interjections from

Adras, Odris and Ebbitt, Tal told Zicka and Yazeq about the situation in the Castle, and how they had followed Sharrakor back to Aenir to stop him from undoing the Forgetting.

"So you see we must kill Sharrakor soon," finished Milla as Tal paused. "We cannot allow him to free every Aeniran and lead them back to our world. We hope you can tell us where he is, or will be."

Zicka and Yazeq looked at each other and spoke in a rapid tumble of words that all seemed to run together.

"This is disturbing news," said Zicka. "We had thought Sharrakor – or Skerrako as he was sometimes called by your ancestors – was still imprisoned beneath the ruins of Rorn."

"Imprisoned?" asked Tal. "How?"

"He was bound into a single shape by Asteyr, who died in the doing of it, then was overcome by Danir, Susir and Grettir," said Kurshken. "They did not wish to slay him, for he was an honourable enemy in their thinking. They bound him in chains of ethren, the golden metal, far beneath the ruins of his city. Someone must have released him, though I am surprised that even a shaper could live so long."

"The Empress and her brother, I guess," said Tal, shaking his head. "Looking for some power to help them overcome the Emperor Mercur."

"He will not be as strong as he was so long ago," continued Zicka. "Which is as well for all of us who would remain free. Sharrakor will not forget that we aided Asteyr and her daughters, and Ramellan too, for that matter. And he will have many to help him, if he undoes the Forgetting and frees them from their bounds."

"So where *will* he undo the Forgetting?" asked Milla.

"There is only one place," replied Zicka. "The Old Khamsoul. It usually inhabits the deserts a day or so south of here, but I will find out where it was last seen."

He called out in the complex language, and a slightly smaller lizard popped its head in. There was a quick exchange, then the other lizard withdrew.

"The Old Khamsoul is possibly the most ancient

entity on Aenir," said Zicka. "It knows all secrets, all names. Sharrakor will need the names of all those bound by the Forgetting in order to release them. The names, and a source of power."

"What power?" asked Milla.

"The Violet Keystone will do," replied Yazeq. "Or the half of it."

"So we have to find out where the Old Khamsoul is," said Tal. "Then go there and stop Sharrakor."

"Go there and *kill* him," said Milla. "Danir should have killed him long ago."

"There is a difficulty you should know," said Zicka. "A most grievous difficulty, I fear."

Everyone looked at the little lizard.

"Sharrakor will be actually *inside* the Old Khamsoul."

"Inside?" asked Crow. "What do you mean *inside*?"

"The Old Khamsoul," explained Zicka, "is a whirlwind. A whirlwind of dust and spinning stones."

"A whirlwind?" Tal shook his head. "Great."

"The whirlwind may not be part of the Old Khamsoul, but merely some form of protective layer," said Yazeq. "There is a pillar of stone at the centre of the whirlwind and some argue that this is in fact the Old Khamsoul. But no one knows for sure."

"If Sharrakor can get into the whirlwind, so can we," said Milla.

Zicka's tongue flickered in and out in agitation.

"No," he said. "The flesh would be stripped from your bones. It is not possible to enter unless the Old Khamsoul allows you. It would not grant that permission if Sharrakor is already there. It never allows more than one being to consult with it at any time."

"There must be *some* way," Tal protested.

"A Shield Maiden thinks of all things possible and expected, then does the impossible and unexpected," said Odris unexpectedly from above their heads. "I know a way into the heart of the Old Khamsoul."

"Odris knows a way," repeated Adras smugly.

"How?" asked Tal and Milla at the same time.

"It's a whirlwind," said Odris. "You don't fly *into* a whirlwind. You get above it and fly down through the eye."

"But the Old Khamsoul is no ordinary whirlwind," cautioned Zicka. "It reaches up to the very margin of the world, high above the clouds. How could you fly above the whirlwind?"

Odris sniffed.

"We can fly higher than anything, if we feel like it," she said. "Up and up and up, and then... a dive straight down through the eye."

"I have climbed high mountains," said Yazeq.

"With height comes cold, and there is little air to breathe. You Storm Shepherds may fly high, but your companions would die."

"No we wouldn't," said Milla. "We could make globes of air with green light and warm ourselves with our Sunstones."

"I do not have a Sunstone," said Malen quietly.

"You may use mine," said Ebbitt. He slipped off the Sunstone he wore in a silver ring and held it out to Malen. "I am afraid that I cannot come with you any further, children."

Malen protested, and Tal started to say something, but Ebbitt dropped the ring in Malen's lap and held up his hand to Tal.

"I am very old and very tired," he said firmly. "And I would undoubtedly lose my false teeth if I went diving into whirlwinds, and with them any dignity I have left. I have almost every confidence in your ability to deal with Sharrakor without my help."

"You don't have false teeth," said Tal.

"That is totally irrelevant," answered Ebbitt. "Now I am going to go to sleep. Good luck."

With that, the old Chosen curled up on one of the thicker rugs and closed his eyes. Tal half expected to see his maned cat slink in and curl up next to him.

Milla and Malen both slowly clapped their fists and then made a sign the others didn't know, crossing their palms one above the other and then gesturing out towards Ebbitt.

"What was that for?" asked Tal.

"He prepares to go to the Ice, in his own way," said Milla. "We honour him."

"He's just tired, that's all," insisted Tal. "Just tired. He's not going to die. Crow, you know him. He's just tired."

"Yes," agreed Crow, but Tal did not know who he was agreeing with. The Freefolk boy did not meet his eyes.

Tal looked back out at the entrance to the roro. He could remember so many times he had gone to Ebbitt, seeking help and advice, or simply to hide away from trouble. It was Ebbitt he had gone to when his father had disappeared, when he had to find a Sunstone...

But he could not let himself grieve now. Ebbitt might have decided to die, but that didn't mean he would.

"Look after my great-uncle, please, Zicka," he said, looking back at Milla, Malen and Crow. "Perhaps... perhaps he will be better in the morning. When we return."

He tried to say the last three words with the confidence of an Emperor, but it did not come out as well as he would have liked. There was an unspoken *if* hanging in the air instead of that *when*.

If we return...

"We'd better plan how we are actually going to do this," said Tal. "Adras, Odris, are you prepared to risk yourselves flying into the eye of the whirlwind?"

"Yes," said Odris. She nudged Adras and he repeated her answer.

"Will we be able to take a boat of light through?"

"No," said Odris. "But we could take it above the eye, then I can carry two if we're just dropping straight down."

The Storm Shepherd's answer chilled the air for a moment as they all visualised dropping straight down the eye of a whirlwind, a whirlwind that rose higher than any mountain.

"We will have the added advantage of surprise," said Milla. "We will be able to strike at Sharrakor before he even suspects we are there. If we manage to actually drop *on* him—"

A lizard poked its head in and babbled something before she could continue.

"The Old Khamsoul is indeed in the Hrykan Desert," said Zicka. "Two days' march away for one of us."

"A few hours' flying," said Milla. "We could be there by the time the sun falls. What is that time called?"

"Dusk," replied Tal.

"A good time to attack," replied Milla with satisfaction. "We will surprise Sharrakor and I will cut his throat with the Talon."

Zicka and Yazeq exchanged a look. Yazeq's tongue flickered sideways.

"Please excuse me," said the older lizard. "There

is something I must attend to."

"If we're going to get there by nightfall I'd better give Malen some lessons on how to use Ebbitt's... *her* Sunstone," said Tal. "Then I guess we'd better make some globes of air. Though... I don't suppose there's any point in waiting until early in the morning and attacking at dawn?"

"Waiting feeds fear," said Milla. "Courage comes with deeds."

"Let's get it over and done with," added Crow.

"Yes," agreed Malen. "The longer we wait, the more the Veil weakens."

Adras and Odris nodded their agreement, huge heads of cloud bobbing up and down.

"The Kurshken wish you good fortune," said Zicka. "And success."

They came out of the roro an hour later, blinking in the sunshine. All had globes of green light around their heads, and Malen kept flinching slightly as warmth flowed in waves out of the Sunstone on her finger and on to her skin.

Tal was surprised to see hundreds of Kurshken massed in the field in front of them. As they emerged, the lizards gave a deep-throated cry and waved their bows in the air.

"What is this?" asked Milla as four Kurshken advanced bearing an ornately carved stone box between them. They knelt before her and offered her the box.

"We are returning something," said Zicka. "Please open the box, Milla."

Milla lifted off the lid and handed it to some more Kurshken who rushed forward. Her hand hovered above the box, an expression of surprise and wonder fleeting across her face before it was suppressed, as she tried to suppress all signs of emotion.

"What is it?" asked Tal, craning his neck.

Milla didn't answer, but she reached in and pulled out a small, shining nail of Violet crystal, the twin to the one she already wore. Milla slipped it on to the forefinger of her right hand and felt the band constrict and become secure.

"The other Talon of Danir," whispered Malen in awe.

"One Danir gave to Ramellan," said Yazeq. "The other she gave into our care. Now we give it back to her daughter's-daughter's-daughter, unto the fortieth generation."

"It is a good omen," declared Milla, holding her hands up in the air so that both Talons caught the sun, glittering violet and gold. "Now we go to slay Sharrakor!"

The Kurshken shouted and drummed their paws, sending water splashing up around them in bold fountains. Milla and Tal led the way down an avenue between splashing and shouting Kurshken, out to the field where they had landed, and where a space was being kept for the re-creation of the flying boat of light.

"Are you sure you can make it by yourself?" whispered Milla as Tal raised his hand and focused on his Sunstone.

Tal nodded and began to work. Soon the keel of the boat began to shimmer on the water, and ribs curved up and out. Planks of yellow started to weave between the ribs and blue traces arched up into the sky, where they were grabbed by the waiting Storm Shepherds.

"Let's go," said Tal, without looking around. He had to keep most of his attention on the boat and his Sunstone.

When everyone was in, Tal changed the focus of the Keystone's power to lift the entire boat up as well as keep it together. With a lurch, the boat rose straight up into the sky, before the Storm

Shepherds were able to drag the traces taut and apply some horizontal force.

Down below, the Kurshken kept splashing and drumming long after the four heroes, the flying boat, and the Storm Shepherds had disappeared from sight. Then they began the process of evacuating Kurshken Corner, to various boltholes and refuges, for they were rational creatures and believed in hedging their bets. They were also lizards of their word, and they carried Ebbitt with them.

It was a long climb to the highest reaches of the atmosphere, to get above the whirlwind that either was or cloaked the Old Khamsoul. It grew colder quickly, but their Sunstones warmed them, and though the air grew thin, they were sustained by their green globes. Tal did worry that they would not last, but he forgot about it as they continued to climb higher and higher and they saw new and strange sights.

First they saw the world curve away beneath them, truly round. Then they broke through cloud and entered another world again, one where the ground beneath them was white and puffy and constantly changing. They rose above great bluffs of sculptured cloud, and then through long wisps of white that could hardly be called clouds at all.

Wind buffeted them mercilessly at some altitudes, only to die away completely as they continued to rise. In any case, the Storm Shepherds could work the wind to some degree, and change both its direction and force. Any wind they could not master they rose above, or passed aside.

Milla saw the Old Khamsoul first and pointed. From far away it looked like a solid spire of stone, reaching up to the heavens through a permanent and very wide hole in the cloud layer, a great circle that declared a no-man's-land around the whirlwind. *Pass here at your peril*, the space seemed to say. *Cross the line and be eaten by the spinning wind.*

"We are so high, and yet it stretches higher still," said Milla. "And down in its heart lies Sharrakor and our destiny."

Her eyes were shining. Tal watched her, catching

glimpses in between focusing on his Sunstone. Truly she was the War-Chief going into battle. He knew there was no such light in his eyes. He just felt scared. Scared that he would die and scared that they would fail. That Sharrakor would kill them and go on to raise his army, return to the Dark World, and finish what he had started.

"Soon!" shouted Odris. "Higher, Tal! Higher!"

"Milla, Crow," said Tal, trying to keep his voice as matter-of-fact as he could. "Blue light into the keel, please. Malen, you just keep yourself warm."

Milla and Crow turned back from the bow where they had both been looking at the Old Khamsoul. They summoned blue light from their Sunstones, sending it pouring into the keel. Tal reinforced it with Violet, and the flying boat shot up sharply, easily keeping pace with the Storm Shepherds' own climb.

"Is it getting warmer?" Malen asked suddenly. "Or am I getting better with my Sunstone?"

Keeping warm with his Sunstone was now so automatic for Tal that he had to concentrate to see how much warmth he was drawing from the stone.

He was surprised to find that he wasn't using it at all, though he certainly had been lower down.

"It gets warmer for a while up this high," shouted Odris. "But it will get colder again. We still have a long way to go."

They climbed in silence for an hour or more then, and once again Tal began to be concerned about the green globes. Theoretically the green glow could contain days' worth of air, but they were rarely used for more than an hour or two. If one of them failed now, it would be impossible to do anything. There had to be air around to compress it into the globe in the first place.

They were close to the Old Khamsoul now, the bare patch in the clouds far below them. They were near enough to see that the whirlwind was not made of dark cloud, but solid particles so that it appeared not grey, but black as night upon the Ice. The whirlwind was made visible by dust and rocks and whatever else it had snatched up, all spinning furiously, far faster than the flying boat or even the Storm Shepherds at their swiftest. Anything that it sucked in would be instantly destroyed. Flesh would be torn from bone, all moisture sucked from a magical cloud. Death would be instantaneous, for human or Storm Shepherd.

The whirlwind was broad at the top, Tal was relieved to see. But then it drew in closer and closer, funnelling air down to what looked like a very narrow tube near the ground. Tal could only trust that the eye would be wide enough down there for them to get through without being ripped apart.

"Higher!" shouted Odris and once again the Sunstones shone brighter and the flying boat lurched up.

"We're higher than the whirlwind!" announced Malen, who was looking over the side.

"We need to get quite a lot higher," said Tal, who had only just realised what they would have to do. "Because when we dissolve the boat, the Storm Shepherds will have to swoop down and catch us before we get blown off track and sucked into... into that."

He pointed over the side and everyone snatched a brief look at the churning vortex of darkness.

"Ready!" shouted Odris as the boat passed the

very centre of the whirlwind, the top of the vortex about five hundred stretches below. She and Adras kept the tension on the traces so that the wind could not blow the boat off station.

"This is it, then," said Tal. His throat was so dry the words came out in a deep Kurshkenlike croak. His heart was hammering so fast it felt like it was shifting position inside his chest.

"Tal, Milla," said Crow suddenly as they all took deep breaths, "if anything... if I don't survive... remember the Underfolk. Remember our freedom."

"I swear it," said Milla. Even her voice sounded strained and strange.

"I will remember," Tal whispered. "Everyone ready? Odris? Adras?"

"Yes!" came the answer, from Freefolk, Icecarls and Storm Shepherds.

"Go!" shouted Tal.

He fired a burst of Violet that dissolved the boat of light around them, and suddenly they were falling, falling much too quickly towards the vortex, as the Storm Shepherds spun around and hurled themselves down as fast as they had ever flown.

29

As Tal fell he grew strangely calm. He had fallen before, in darkness and cold, on another world. That had been the beginning of everything, in a way, and now maybe this was the end. Whichever way it went, it was the end. Maybe Adras wouldn't catch him and he would plummet to his death, or the wind would take him out of the eye, into the reach of the whirling destruction of the Old Khamsoul, or Sharrakor would laugh and slay him in an instant. But he would have done his best. His father would be proud, he knew, and his mother. And not just his parents. He had done many good and great things, just like the Sword Thanes of

Icecarl legend, in the songs that always ended with them being brought home dead. After they had defeated the enemy, of course. So he had to defeat Sharrakor...

Milla fell with thoughts of what was going to happen next. She had no doubt Odris would catch her, Odris being able to fly faster than anything could fall. Sharrakor was Milla's concern. He had surprised her in the Chamber of the Veil, with an attack she could not counter. What if he had more tricks, more secret weapons? What tactics could she employ, other than the surprise of falling from the sky?

Crow fell silently, his thoughts, as always, of the long struggle to free his people. Fashnek was no more, but the Hall of Nightmares still stood. The Chosen would be defeated by the Icecarls, and he trusted the Icecarls to stand by their word. But the greater danger to the Underfolk was themselves. They had been held in servitude so long that it would be hard for them to come out of it. But there were Freefolk to help them, provided that Sharrakor did not win and kill everyone. Perhaps, he thought, what the Underfolk needed most of all was something – or someone – to believe in. So they knew that an Underfolk could be the equal of any Chosen…

Malen fell with the mental discipline of a Crone. She emptied her mind of all thoughts and simply acted as a recorder. This was an experience all the Crones would wish to share, and she only regretted that she could not reach the others to share it immediately. But if she survived, many would want to walk in her memories, to see Aenir and to fall forty thousand stretches down the eye of a whirlwind…

The next thought all four of them had was overwhelming relief as strong cloud arms closed around their waists. They were still falling, but under control, Adras holding Tal under one arm and Crow under the other, Odris with Milla and Malen clutched close to her chest.

The roar of the air rushing past and the constant din of the whirlwind made it impossible to talk as they fell, even if they had wanted to. Every now and then someone would gasp as they looked below and it seemed as if the eye had narrowed too much for them to get through, but a few seconds later they would find that it was all an illusion. The eye did narrow, but it was always at least a hundred stretches wide, which looked like nothing from very high above.

They were falling for so long that it was a surprise when they suddenly saw the rocky spire that was the heart of the Old Khamsoul, and the desert ground below it. Tal's calm disappeared in an instant, to be replaced by panic. The top of the spire was flat, but it was no larger than the deck of an iceship and they had to land on it.

That landing space grew closer with awful rapidity. Tal saw a bright shape upon it, a shining blot impossible to make out, but he knew it was Sharrakor. The blot grew larger and sharper, and became a dragon, a dragon that shone like a mirror in what little sunlight came down the vortex from above.

All four of them screamed in the last second, joining with the booming shouts of the Storm Shepherds. Tal screamed in a mixture of fear and anger, Milla screamed a war cry, Crow screamed for his people, and Malen didn't even know she was screaming.

They hit the rocky surface of the spire harder than expected. Tal fell over, rolled once, thought of the edge and stopped. Milla landed on her feet, both Talons already extended, whips of light dancing from her hands. Crow landed well too, and had his Sunstone in his hand. Malen smacked her knee and doubled into a ball to clutch at it, but it did not stop her from beginning the Prayer to Asteyr, her voice and gaze directed straight at the dragon who reared up at the other end of the spire.

For a second, Sharrakor kept speaking names out into the vortex, his half of the Violet Keystone pulsing where he held it dwarfed and tiny in one enormous claw.

Milla dashed forward as Sharrakor turned. She struck with the Talons, light streaking out to lash at the dragon's forelimbs. But Sharrakor flapped his wings and rose above her, and the Violet Keystone flashed red.

Tal sat up and interposed a Violet Shield of

Discontinuity between Sharrakor and Milla. A moment later a Red Ray flashed out, hit the shield and disappeared.

Sharrakor flew higher, as Milla leaped and lashed out again, her twin lassos of light barely missing his tail. Crow shot a Red Ray up at the dragon, and Tal fired too, but both were met by a blue defensive shimmer that Tal didn't know. He changed to a blast of pure Indigo, but that too was countered, and still Sharrakor flew up, until he was beyond the reach of Crow's Sunstone. Tal knew his own spells would be too weak.

The Storm Shepherds rose up after the dragon, roaring a challenge. Tal couldn't hear what they said, but Sharrakor's voice was clear, penetrating even the constant drone of the whirlwind that surrounded them all.

"Emechis! Gheshthil arrok Adras! Gheshthil arrok Odris!"

The Storm Shepherds screamed. Both stalled, hanging in the air for an instant. Then they dropped as if they were suddenly made of stone rather than cloud. As they fell, they were sucked sideways towards the whirlwind – and certain destruction.

"No!" screamed Tal. He raised his Sunstone and, without thinking, sent out two shimmering clouds of pure Violet. They enveloped Adras and Odris a second before the two Storm Shepherds were ruthlessly sucked into the spinning wall of debris. The Violet cocoons were visible for a moment, then they were gone.

Tal had no idea what he had done, whether it had worked, or if Adras and Odris had survived. He had no time to think about it either, as Sharrakor sent a beam of Indigo into the whirlwind, plucked out a giant, jagged stone and sent it hurtling down towards them.

Once again Tal acted instinctively. He made an instant Hand of Light from pure Violet and tried to slap the missile away, at the same time that Crow hit it with a Red Ray of Destruction. But the Hand was too weak, merely deflecting the rock, and the Red Ray only scored its surface.

The rock hit the edge of the spire and splintered into thousands of pieces of deadly shrapnel. Everyone threw themselves to the ground, and Tal just managed to raise a Shield of Discontinuity in time. Even though they weren't hit, the missile had served as a distraction.

Sharrakor followed the missile down, swooping with his wings folded, only spreading them to brake at the last second. He struck Tal in the back with a foreclaw as the Chosen boy sprang back up, and knocked Milla over with a sweep of his mighty tail. Crow managed to roll aside from the dragon's other claw, and Malen was ignored as she lay on the edge of the spire, still bravely chanting the Prayer to Asteyr.

Tal felt blood running down his back as he struggled to turn over. But Sharrakor was too quick, and even as Tal got free and raised his hand, the claw came smashing down, pinning him to the rock. Milla was pinned too, caught in the rapidly tightening coils of the dragon's tail, the Talons of Danir held too close to her own body to be used.

Crow ducked under the dragon's body and fired a Red Ray at point-blank range. But the beam splashed across the dragon's mirrorlike scales, and Sharrakor laughed. His mighty jaws snapped down as Crow stood fearlessly firing Ray after Ray into the creature's open mouth.

Crow ducked as the dragon struck. The terrible jaws closed, but not entirely on air. The hood of Crow's robe was caught. Sharrakor lifted him up and twitched his head, and the Freefolk boy was sent flying into oblivion.

Tal closed his eyes, only to open them again a moment later as Malen's voice rose to a shout on the last word of the Prayer to Asteyr, and the weight on his chest disappeared.

The dragon had vanished. In its place was a man. Or a manlike creature, for his skin was still mirror-scaled and his eyes were the deep black eyes of Sharrakor. He held the half of the Violet Keystone, which he used casually to fire a Red Ray at Malen. The Ray hit her as she rushed to attack, a lump of rock in her hand. The Ray seared across her legs and she tumbled over, almost to the edge of the spire.

"Inconvenient," said Sharrakor as he walked over to the Crone and raised the Keystone again. "Release me, Crone, so that I may take my grander shape, and I will let you live."

"No," said Malen. She started to speak again, but Sharrakor set his foot upon her throat.

Tal tried to raise his hand, to point his Sunstone at Sharrakor, but a familiar pain intervened. His arm was dislocated again, and useless.

"Milla!" shrieked Tal. "Kill him!"

But Milla was lying unconscious – or dead – twenty stretches away, the breath squeezed out of her by Sharrakor's tail.

Tal reached across with his good arm, dragged his right hand across his chest and started to pull off the Sunstone ring. The movement attracted Sharrakor's attention. He raised his foot from Malen's throat and turned, his own Sunstone flashing red.

Tal screamed with pain as he jerked his useless right hand up so he could see into his Sunstone. He summoned Violet and raised a shield as Sharrakor's Red Ray struck.

The Red Ray snapped off. Through the Violet glow of his shield, Tal saw Sharrakor stalk off to one side. Ignoring the pain in his shoulder, Tal rolled around as well, and moved the shield just as another Red Ray snapped out.

Sharrakor laughed and began to walk back in the other direction. Tal groaned in pain and misery. Sharrakor was playing with him, moving too quickly for Tal to be able to do anything but defend. But he had to do something. He was the only one left.

Then Tal saw a slight movement from Milla. She was moving her head very slowly so she could see what Sharrakor was doing. And she was looking at something behind him...

For a second Tal lost concentration and his shield wavered. Sharrakor immediately fired a Red Ray, and laughed again as Tal only just managed to get the shield back up.

In that moment of lost concentration Tal had seen something that gave him hope. Crow had climbed back up over the edge of the spire and was right behind Sharrakor. The Freefolk boy had something clutched in his hand, but it was too small to be a knife and Tal could not see his Sunstone.

Crow crept closer to Sharrakor. Tal groaned again, louder, to distract Sharrakor. If the Aeniran turned now, he would blast Crow before he could do anything.

Crow was three steps away... two... Tal saw Milla tense... one step... Tal let his shield down and screamed, and Milla jumped up shouting. Crow leaped upon the enemy, wrapping his legs around Sharrakor's waist and his left arm around his neck while with his right hand he smashed a small bottle into Sharrakor's face and a dark fluid splattered everywhere.

Tal stared as a clear fluid dripped down Sharrakor's face, and for that instant, he wondered what Crow had done. Then he recognised the sickly scent of caveroach poison, poison that was death to touch. But was it still poisonous in Aenir?

Tal was answered by a scream from Sharrakor, a scream that cut through all other sound, that intensified and grew louder and louder until Tal had to push his finger in one ear and grind the other against the stone to keep out the sound. Milla clapped her hands to her ears, the Talons sending crazy lines of light around her head like a halo.

The scream stopped as suddenly as it had begun, Sharrakor scraping at his own face as he and Crow teetered on the very edge of the spire. But while Sharrakor fought to wipe the poison away, the Freefolk boy did not. He fought only to take the Sunstone from Sharrakor's hands, and when he had it, he threw it towards Tal.

As the Sunstone flew through the air, Crow threw his arms back. Locked together with Sharrakor, the two teetered on the brink, an image caught forever in Tal's mind.

Then they fell, Crow's final cry cut off as the poison did its fatal work.

"Freeeeedom! Free—"

30

Tal crawled to the edge of the spire and looked down. Far below, on the red desert sands, he could see a speck of black still wrapped around something that glittered and glowed.

Milla bent over him and gripped his wrist and elbow. Tal gritted his teeth, but could not help crying out as she put his arm back into the shoulder socket.

"He was brave," said Milla quietly. "Brave as any Icecarl, as any Sword Thane of legend."

"First of the Freefolk," whispered Tal. "He saved us all, in the end. With caveroach poison..."

He started to laugh, but it turned into a sob, a

sob that racked his whole body until he managed to get himself under control. Then he felt tired, more tired than he had ever been. He just wanted to lie down and sleep for years. They had defeated Sharrakor. Let someone else take over now...

But he was not left to lie there. Milla helped him up and practically dragged him across to where Malen lay. She was so still that fear struck Tal again.

"Is she..."

"She lives," replied Milla. "Her throat is bruised and she is burned, but I have put a healing light upon that. She will wake soon."

Tal looked at her. "An Underfolk defeats a monster, an Icecarl wields Light Magic," he said. "And a Chosen doesn't know what to do – except look for Adras and Odris. But how do we get out of this old whirlwind?"

"We all have to return to the Castle," said Milla. "The Veil must be restored, and peace made between all our peoples. That is what we must do."

"Yes," replied Tal. "And we must free the Underfolk."

He looked down at the half Keystone Crow had thrown to him, and slid it upon the finger where he wore the half Keystone Milla had given him. As the two Sunstones met, there was an intense flash of Violet, a stinging pain in Tal's finger. The ring was whole once more, the Sunstones become one.

"You can help us all get back to the Castle from here, can't you?" asked Milla.

Tal did not hear her. He was staring down at the Violet Keystone, lost in its depths.

Milla smacked him on the back and repeated her question.

"What? No. That is, I don't know..." began Tal. Then he stopped to think about it and was surprised to find inside himself an absolute confidence that he *could* lead them back from anywhere in Aenir. "Yes. I suppose we can go from here. You'd better wake up Malen. I'm just going... for a walk."

Milla frowned. There was nowhere to walk to, atop the spire. But she bent down and propped Malen up against herself, wincing as her bruised ribs and back complained.

Tal walked to where Sharrakor had stood, right on the edge of the spire. The rock was worn glassy smooth there, as if by many feet. It would be treacherous if it was wet, but Tal guessed it never rained here, in the heart of the whirlwind.

"Khamsoul!" he shouted. "I have a question."

The sound of the whirlwind did not change, but somehow Tal heard a quiet voice above it, a voice that was old and slow and mellow, gentle and vaguely amused at the same time.

"Of course you do, Tal Graile-Rerem, Emperor of the Chosen of the Castle. I will grant you one question, and one answer."

"Did you kill Adras and Odris?"

"I do not kill my children," breathed the Old Khamsoul. "Even my children's-children's-children, beyond the count of years. They live, and now know their ancestry. You may ask another question."

"Could... could I have done anything differently?" asked Tal. "Was there some way to do everything better? To defeat Sharrakor, without Crow... without Crow dying, or Jarek... or all the other people, all the Aenirans?"

"I cannot answer that," whispered the whirlwind. "I can only say what is, and what has been, not what might have been or what might come to pass. You may ask another question."

Tal stared out at the whirlwind.

"Who started the war between our worlds?" he asked.

"Which one?" The Old Khamsoul sighed. "Which one? There have been so many wars. And even I cannot always say how they began."

Tal was silent.

"I have not answered. Do you have another question?"

"No," said Tal slowly. "I do not know what to ask. I will come back someday, if you let me."

"You may come," said the Old Khamsoul. "I shall be here."

Tal turned and walked back to Milla and Malen. A minute later, three Sunstones flashed, and three voices spoke the Way to the Dark World. A rainbow shone, and the spire of the Old Khamsoul was empty.

EPILOGUE

The Great Gate of the Castle had been shut for more than a thousand years. Now the vast gate of golden metal stood open to the Dark World beyond. But it was not dark, for in the Hall of Welcome a thousand Sunstones shone, and out on the road beyond there were scores more Sunstones, hundreds of moth lanterns and many oil-soaked torches burning with blue flames.

Tal stood in front of a crowd of Chosen and Freefolk. He was clad in simple white robes rather than violet, though the Violet Keystone shining on his hand splashed him with colour. His natural shadow fell on the floor behind him. Only natural shadows flickered among this gathering, though there were still renegade Chosen, their Spiritshadows and free shadows elsewhere in the Castle.

Opposite Tal, in front of a throng of Icecarls, stood Milla. The Talons of Danir glowed violet on her fingers, and the crown on her head was newly polished. Her Selski hide armour had been repaired and cleaned, and once more she wore her Merwin-horn sword at her side. She also wore a Sunstone ring, which shone indigo and was larger than the half Keystone she had given up.

"Farewell, at least for a circling," said Milla, clapping her fists together in a gesture to Tal. "Or more, perhaps. We will be busy."

Tal nodded in understanding. Though they had saved the Veil, it had been temporarily weakened, causing a shift in temperature and changing both the weather and the Ice. The pattern of Selski migration had altered, and with that alteration had come many conflicts among the Icecarl clans who had to depart from their traditional routes and hunting grounds. As always, the Crones would decide these disputes, but they had asked Milla to assist in their decisions. She would lead a special force of Shield Maidens and Crones who were to circumnavigate the world, ruling on the new boundaries and prerogatives.

"I'll be busy too," he sighed. Despite the collapse of the old regime, the vast majority of Chosen had still acclaimed him as Emperor. The Freefolk, led by Crow's brother Bennem – who had been cured by the Crones – had agreed to that acclamation, provided he was called Emperor of the Castle, not just the Chosen.

Tal, mindful of his promise to Crow, had accepted for the time being. Now he had the task of trying to make the new society work. It was a tall order when within the Castle there were rebel Chosen, recalcitrant Chosen who didn't want to do anything useful, former Underfolk who couldn't imagine change, and Freefolk who were bitter and wanted the Chosen to serve them or to be punished for their past.

"I wish Ebbitt—" Tal began to say, when he was interrupted by a scrawny, rather stooped Icecarl who seemed to be having difficulty with his face mask.

"Wish what?" said the Icecarl, lifting the mask to reveal a familiar long nose. "Wish I'd been bored to death by those Kurshkens?"

"No," Tal said, embracing his great-uncle. "You know what I wish."

"Hmmph," snorted Ebbitt. "I'll be back. Couldn't miss this opportunity, you know. There I was, on my last breath... or perhaps the second-last breath, I can't be sure... and I thought if I die now I'll never see the Ice. Beside, there's those Crones. I like the sound of them."

Tal let Ebbitt go, but pressed two fingers against his great-uncle's chest. Something moved under the furs, something other than skin and bone.

"Ebbitt!"

"What can I say?" exclaimed Ebbitt. "It wants to come with me. We've been playing Beastmaker and I'm winning a hundred and six games to one hundred and eight."

The Codex beat against Ebbitt's chest and the old man hastily added, "The count is a little in dispute. It could be one hundred and six even."

Tal frowned. The Codex was too valuable to lose. But there was no guarantee he'd be able to consult it even if it did stay in the Castle. At least if it was with Ebbitt he'd be able to find it when he had to. Besides, Malen was going to stay in the Castle and several other Crones were going to join her, as part of a permanent embassy. Tal would be able to communicate with Ebbitt and the Codex via the Crones.

And with Milla, too. There would be much to talk about.

"Farewell, Milla," said Tal. He held out his wrist, showing the scars of the oaths they had made together. Milla bared her wrist, and they touched scars, cool skin against cool skin.

Milla smiled, a smile that Tal had not seen before. He smiled back and looked into her eyes. In their joined gaze, they both saw everything they had been through together, from their meeting on the Ice to the fall of Sharrakor.

Everyone was silent as they stood together. Time ticked over in Icecarl breaths and Chosen seconds, counted in sparks within their Sunstones. Finally, Milla raised her hand and Tal's fell away.

Milla held her hand high above her head. A Talon flared and a violet whip spun overhead, before falling into motes of light as Milla closed her fist and lowered her arm.

Icecarls shouted, their calls reverberating through the great hall. Then they shouldered their burdens and set out on the long road down the Mountain of Light. Down towards the Ice and the Living Sea of Selski, down to their windborne homes, the clan ships of the Icecarls.

Milla did not look back.

Tal watched for a moment, then turned towards the shining Sunstones, to the thousands of halls and rooms and corridors of the Chosen and the Freefolk, the people of the Castle.

But even as friends and strangers alike came to his side to ask questions or beg favours or tell him things, his thoughts were only on one small part of the Castle. A suite of rooms with the front door marked by an Orange Sthil-beast leaping over a seven-pointed star.

Beyond that door his family was together again. His father, Rerem, who had been rescued from the Orange Keystone, was regaining both his sanity and his strength. His mother, Graile, had almost totally recovered from the water-spider poison. His brother, Gref, had been cured so rapidly by the Crones that he had already got into several sorts of minor trouble. And Tal's little sister, Kusi, seemed to have forgotten that anything had happened at all.

Tal smiled again, a smile tinged with the weight of memory and responsibility. So much *had* happened, and so much lay ahead.

But everything could wait, thought Tal, as he made his way through the crowd.

For Tal Graile-Rerem was finally going home, and he had a Sunstone.